Hamilton was admittedly impressed that the detective seemed to have all the bases covered, giving them their best shot at locating Juliet.

He just wondered if it would be enough. "Well, I thank you for your current and future efforts, Annette."

"It's my job, Hamilton," she stressed. "With any luck, your niece simply lost her bearings, as young people tend to do these days, and will be totally embarrassed about it when she gets home and tries to explain."

He grinned, hoping she was right and they could celebrate Christmas as planned. Though he almost found himself hating to leave the detective's office, Hamilton knew it was time he did just that. "I won't take up any more of your time," he told her, getting to his feet.

Annette stood too, offering him a smile. "I understand how stressful something like this can be, especially at this time of year. If you want to give me your number, I can keep you informed on where this goes."

Hamilton gave her his cell phone number and was given hers in return, which he added to his contacts.

"As soon as we hear anything concrete," Annette said, "I'll let you know."

"Thanks." He met her eyes and realized that she had extended a hand. Shaking it, Hamilton noticed how soft her skin felt against his. Releasing the surprisingly firm grip Annette displayed, he showed himself out, while sensing her watching him leave.

To H. Loraine, the love of my life and best friend, whose support has been unwavering through the many wonderful years together. To my dear mother, Marjah Aljean, who gave me the tools to pursue my passions in life, including writing fiction for publication; and for my loving sister, Jacquelyn, who helped me become the person I am today. To the loyal fans of my romance, mystery, suspense and thriller fiction published over the years. Lastly, a nod goes out to my wonderful editors, Allison Lyons and Denise Zaza, for the great opportunity to lend my literary voice and creative spirit to the successful Harlequin Intrigue line.

CHRISTMAS LIGHTS KILLER

R. Barri Flowers

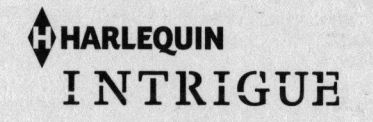

H HARLEQUIN®
INTRIGUE™

Recycling programs
for this product may
not exist in your area.

ISBN-13: 978-1-335-59053-4

Christmas Lights Killer

For questions and comments about the quality of this book,
please contact us at CustomerService@Harlequin.com.

Harlequin Enterprises ULC
22 Adelaide St. West, 41st Floor
Toronto, Ontario M5H 4E3, Canada
www.Harlequin.com

Printed in U.S.A.

R. Barri Flowers is an award-winning author of crime, thriller, mystery and romance fiction featuring three-dimensional protagonists, riveting plots, unexpected twists and turns, and heart-pounding climaxes. With an expertise in true crime, serial killers and characterizing dangerous offenders, he is perfectly suited for the Harlequin Intrigue line. Chemistry and conflict between the hero and heroine, attention to detail and incorporating the very latest advances in criminal investigations are the cornerstones of his romantic suspense fiction. Discover more on popular social networks and Wikipedia.

Visit the Author Profile page at Harlequin.com.

CAST OF CHARACTERS

Annette Lynley—A Dabs County Sheriff's Department detective on the hunt for a strangler serial killer in Carol Creek. Will the handsome trooper assisting on the case be a distraction or welcomed presence?

Hamilton McCade—An Indiana State senior trooper in search of his missing niece. Will finding her take away from the growing attraction for the lead detective and desire to protect her from harm?

Will Hossack—A detective for the sheriff's department who is committed to solving murders, whatever it takes.

Patrick and Paul DeLuca—These brothers run a Christmas tree farm and are currently suspects in the case. Could either be the Christmas Lights Killer?

Kelly Okamoto—A forensic scientist, she is determined to help crack the case. But can she?

The Christmas Lights Killer—This unsub uses string lights to strangle female victims in town and targets Annette to add to the list of victims.

Prologue

His seemed like a friendly enough face. She could maybe even call it handsome. The eyes were crystal blue and a good fit above a Greek nose and a slightly crooked mouth. His triangular face had a square jawline and a dark chinstrap beard. Dark brown or black hair was in a messy, tapered style that seemed to suit him. Like her, he was casually dressed for winter weather in early December, wearing a blue hooded parka jacket, tech jeans, black leather gloves and brown steel-toe boots. The fact that he just happened along in his black Ford Bronco Sport Big Bend didn't faze her. How could he have known that her own red Honda Insight would just conk out on the side of the road, leaving her few options, given that she couldn't seem to get a signal on her cell phone.

So, when he offered her a ride to the nearest service station, JoBeth Sorenson threw caution to the wind and accepted graciously. The fact that it was Christmas time and most people in the town of Carol Creek, Indiana, seemed festive and in the holiday spirit gave her further reason for believing that accepting a ride from a total stranger would bring her no harm. After getting into the front seat and buckling up, JoBeth grinned at the man who never identified himself, but offered her a generous, toothy smile. He was playing some Christmas music, which again made it seem like he was anything but a grinch out to ruin her holiday. She wished the same were true for her ex-boyfriend, Aaron Heathcote. They'd broken up two weeks ago, after he confessed to cheating on her, validating what she had suspected for a while but chosen to ignore it till she couldn't any longer. Being single again right before Christmas wasn't exactly her idea of jingle bells ringing. But she supposed it was best that she knew the truth before the new year, giving her the opportunity for a fresh start as a suddenly available high school English teacher.

They drove down the snow-covered road for a full minute with neither uttering a word, as JoBeth was totally wrapped up in her thoughts. Only when she noticed that they had passed by Walker Street, which would take them toward the service station, did she face the driver with mild concern. "I think we missed our turn," she said, flipping her long, multilayered blond hair to the side.

"Really?" He glanced at her and back to the road. "Sorry about that," he claimed. "Don't know what I was thinking. I'll turn around up ahead and we'll go back."

"Thank you." JoBeth breathed a sigh of relief. Maybe he really was a nice guy after all. And not her worst nightmare. She even imagined that, judging by his looks and seemingly not much older than her twenty-seven years of age, he might even be good boyfriend material. Assuming he too was single and available, once they got past her current predicament.

"No problem," he said.

She smiled. "So, any big holiday plans?" she asked, if only for effect.

"Not really." He glanced at her. "How about you?"

JoBeth considered that her parents would be spending Christmas in Hawaii and her younger sister, Dana, had decided to go skiing with her boyfriend at the Paoli Peaks alpine ski resort in Orange County, Indiana, nearly one hundred miles away. That left JoBeth's best friend, Mariah O'Sullivan. But she had other plans that didn't include her, so JoBeth was honest about it when she responded, "None that I can think of, other than having my car back up and running again."

The man laughed as he turned onto Brockton Drive. "Regarding that… I'm afraid you won't be needing your car again…"

"Excuse me?" She cast her big blue eyes at him with alarm.

He chuckled again and kept driving down the desolate road, away from the homes they had passed by earlier, many decorated for Christmas. "I said that your car won't be of much use to you now."

"I don't understand what you mean."

He gave her a menacing look. "You'll know soon enough."

JoBeth's radar suddenly kicked in, alerting her that something was very off about the driver. How had she not noticed it before? "I think you better let me out here," she insisted. Though farther away from assistance than before, she would rather take her chances of freezing to death than remain in the car with someone who was acting too weird for her comfort.

"I think not," he said in a mocking tone of voice. He pressed down on the accelerator.

She tried to open the passenger-side door, but he had used the master lock to prevent this. "Stop the car and let me out!" she demanded, hoping that would somehow do the trick.

When he brought the vehicle to a halt, while managing to maintain control on the slippery road, the man said, "I did half of what you asked. Unfortunately, the other half won't be possible just yet."

JoBeth yanked on the door handle, desperately trying to force the door open, to no avail. "Let me go!" she snapped, her heart racing.

"No can do," he responded tersely. "Didn't your mother ever teach you to never get into cars with strangers?" He laughed. "If so, you should've listened to her." He reached into the back seat and picked up a string of Christmas lights. "Bet you're wondering what these are for?"

JoBeth didn't even want to imagine what kind of sick games he intended to play with those lights. All she wanted was to some way, somehow, get out of this alive. Was it too late for that? "Please," she begged him. "I just want out. I won't say anything to anyone about this." She wanted to say *kidnapping* or *abduction*, even if it didn't start out that way, seeing that he was now holding her against her will. But she didn't dare antagonize him while he had her at a disadvantage.

"Sorry, but I have to do this and you have no choice but to take it, as you've reached the end of your road, literally," he snorted, and wrapped the string of Christmas lights tightly around her neck.

JoBeth gasped for air as she tried to loosen the copper wire cutting through her neck. She attempted to claw his face, but he somehow managed to keep it just beyond her reach while strangling her forcefully. When she became too weak to fight anymore, her will to live seemed to fade like fog. Before losing consciousness for good, JoBeth was left to wonder how this could have happened to her. And what came next.

HE TWISTED AND tightened the string of Christmas lights around her short neck till she breathed her final breath and her body went limp. How lucky could he have been? He had been searching for the perfect person to kill. And just like that, there she was. Stranded on the side of the road, looking to trust whoever came along to assist in her time of need. Good thing for him that he beat someone else to the punch in offering to drive her to a service station.

Bad thing for her that she accepted his offer and, in the process, signed her own death warrant. He stared at her for a long moment, admiring his almost work of art. In death, she had brought to life his urge to kill. And if he had anything to do with it, she wouldn't be the last. Unless he got stupid and allowed the cops to catch him in the act or afterward. He didn't intend to let that happen.

Unlocking the passenger door, he undid her seat belt, opened the door and shoved the woman's dead body to the side of the road, leaving the Christmas lights around her neck. He closed the door and drove off on his merry way, humming along to the Christmas tune coming from the radio and looking ahead to when he would be able to go down this proverbial road again.

Chapter One

"My daughter's missing!" the woman cried as she stormed into the office of Dabs County Sheriff's Detective Annette Lynley.

Annette had finally gotten comfortable with the small office she was given a year ago, along with a badge and Glock 43 single-stack 9mm pistol, when taking the position within the Sheriff's Department's Detective Bureau, which included three full-time detectives and two reserve deputies. She'd managed to make the office feel more like home on a professional level, having been allowed to replace the age-old furnishings for something more suitable, including a washed-gray L-shaped wooden desk, an ergonomic mesh task chair and upgraded laptop. But there were bigger things on her mind these days. At age thirty-four, apart from feeling the constant need to prove herself as more than capable of handling the job, Annette and her fellow detectives were dealing with some shocking homicides. The crimes were hardly the norm for Dabs County, located in the northern part of Indiana, and the small towns within, including Carol Creek, where the sheriff's department was located on Elm Street. Till recently, drug-related offenses, domestic violence and juvenile delinquency were the main forms of criminality the Detective Bureau or DB was tasked with responding to. Now they had a bona fide serial killer on their hands, with Annette as the lead detective in the investigation. Dubbed by the local press as "The Christmas Lights Killer," thus far the unknown suspect—or unsub—had strangled to death two attractive young women. In each case, the murder weapon was a string of Christmas lights left around the neck of the victim as the perpetrator's chilling calling card. The killings threatened to put a serious damper on the holiday season in the county, with Christmas little more than two weeks away.

As she sat at the desk, Annette's bold brown-and-green eyes sized up the woman, who looked to be in her early forties and was dressed warmly for this time of year. She was on the slender side, around Annette's height of five-seven and a half, with blue eyes and short, blond-brown hair in a feathered cut. Normally, Annette would have expected the office clerk, Patti Gellar, to prevent visitors from getting very far in this section of the department. Someone usually came out to speak with them. But Patti had been given the day off for a doctor's appointment and everyone else was out in the field, leaving only Annette to handle whoever had a problem, for better or worse.

So handle it, Annette told herself. "And you are?" she asked the woman politely.

"Maureen McCade."

"What's your daughter's name?"

"Juliet." Her voice shook. "Juliet McCade."

"How long has she been missing, Mrs. McCade?"

"Please call me Maureen, Detective. There's no husband in the picture." She frowned. "I raised Juliet as a single mom. With the help of my younger brother, Hamilton."

In that moment, Annette couldn't help but reflect on her own upbringing and what might have been. Having been given up for adoption by her unwed mother while still an infant, Annette had been adopted by Oklahomans Taylor and Caroline Lynley, becoming their fourth child behind three birth children, Scott, Madison and Russell. Though they fully embraced her, and Annette couldn't imagine having been a part of any other family, she still wondered sometimes if she and her birth mother might have found a way to get through the difficult times had they stayed together. Perhaps if there had been an uncle around like Maureen's brother Hamilton to help the cause, things may have turned out differently.

"I haven't seen or spoken to Juliet since she went out last night around seven p.m.," Maureen continued, ill at ease, getting Annette's attention again.

Annette glanced at the quartz clock on the wall and saw that it was 11 a.m. Meaning only sixteen hours had passed since Maureen last saw her daughter. Though one was free to report someone missing at any time, the department usually didn't start an investigation for twenty-four hours from the time the person was last seen. Unless they were talking about a minor or a suspected abduction, or had other clear indication that the missing person was in danger. But given the current situation of women turning up dead, no case of a missing female could be taken lightly.

"I know what you're thinking," Maureen said perceptively. "That not enough time has passed for me to be concerned." She sighed. "Well, I know my daughter. Juliet has never stayed out all night without letting me know where she was and who with. Besides, I got a text message from her, in which Juliet thought someone might be following her. I tried texting back, but got no response. Something's wrong. I can feel it."

Annette twisted her lips musingly. "Can I see the text?"

Maureen took the cell phone from the pocket of her quilted jacket and brought up the text message before passing the phone to her. Annette read the text.

Hey, I think I'm being followed by someone. Maybe it's just my imagination.

The message had been sent at seven forty last night. All things considered, it was certainly unnerving to Annette, to say the least. But it wasn't exactly an indication that a crime had taken place. Or who might have committed it. "In most instances of missing persons, they tend to turn up unharmed, sooner or later," she pointed out, knowing full well that this would do little to appease the worried mother. Truthfully, it didn't give Annette much solace, either, as each individual case stood on its own merits.

Maureen rubbed her nose. "I keep trying to tell myself that. But this is so unlike Juliet that I can't help thinking something bad has happened to her."

"Let's not jump to conclusions," Annette cautioned her gingerly, wanting to believe otherwise. "How old is Juliet?"

"Twenty-one."

"And she lives with you?"

"At the moment." Maureen paused and explained, "She's been staying at my house for the last month. Or ever since the lease to her apartment ended and the rent became more than she could afford, in spite of working two part-time jobs."

Annette could relate, having been down that road of struggling to make ends meet in her early adulthood. During her college years and after graduating from the University of Oklahoma with a Bachelor of Arts in Criminology, she had worked her fair share of part-time jobs and lived in low-income housing off campus. Of course, her financial position was secure now, after she'd landed a job in law enforcement. Her late adopted father and mother had been a police chief and criminal court judge respectively; and two of her siblings were FBI special agents and the other a law enforcement ranger. So it was natural that Annette had followed in their footsteps and gotten into police work herself, first working as a deputy sheriff in different locations before becoming a detective with the Dabs County Sheriff's Office.

"Won't you have a seat, Maureen?" Annette

asked her, then watched as the woman sat in one of the two barrel-shaped guest chairs on the other side of the desk. Needing further insight into the missing young woman, Annette inquired, "You said your daughter has two part-time jobs. What are they?"

"During the week, Juliet works as a sales clerk at a boutique in the Carol Creek Shopping Center." Maureen squirmed in the seat. "Recently, she's been working weekends at a Christmas tree lot on Forrester Lane."

Annette didn't see anything unusual about that on the face of it, but made a mental note. "Does Juliet have a boyfriend?" If so, she imagined that the daughter might have gone to his place.

"She recently broke up with her boyfriend, Chad Lawrence," Maureen claimed.

"Is it possible that they got back together?" Annette clasped her hands together.

"No, Juliet dumped him for cheating on her," she insisted, frowning. "Would you go back to a cheater?"

Annette had been put on the spot, uncomfortably. She thought back to the last man she had been involved with—Eric Rodriguez. After dating for nearly a year and believing he could be the one, Annette had discovered that Eric was anything but the one: he'd been having an affair with one of his married colleagues. The experience had left a bitter taste in Annette's mouth and had her wondering if real love and commitment would ever be in the cards for her. "No, I'm pretty sure I wouldn't," she had to admit to Juliet's mother.

"Didn't think so."

Annette gazed at her across the desk. "Maybe Juliet met someone else and decided to spend the night with him," she suggested. "Or otherwise simply lost track of time. Not too uncommon for young adults these days."

Maureen bristled. "I just need to know she's okay."

I'd like to know that, too, Annette thought. "Where was your daughter going when she went out?"

"She was supposed to meet a friend, Rita Getzler, at a local hangout called the Pear Pub. But according to Rita, Juliet never showed up."

"Hmm…" Annette didn't like the sound of that. "Does Juliet have a car?"

"Yes, she bought a Subaru Impreza last summer."

"We'll try and locate it," Annette said. Given the winter conditions, it was entirely possible that Juliet had gotten into an accident and could be hurt—or worse—and unable to communicate. "Have you checked the hospital?" There was only Carol Creek General in town, but one other hospital and some clinics were spread across the county.

"Yes. They don't show a Juliet McCade as having been admitted."

"That's good," Annette told her. At least insofar as no official indication that Juliet had run into harm's way. "It means she isn't necessarily injured." But still cause for concern to be missing at all.

"Not that we know of." Maureen frowned pessimistically. "We need to find her!"

"We will." Annette suspected that this assurance would fall on deaf ears as long as her daughter was still unaccounted for. "Do you have a photo of Juliet?"

Maureen nodded. She pulled it up on her cell phone and showed Annette. "It was taken last week in our living room."

Annette studied the missing young woman. She was biracial, like her, and pretty with brown eyes and long, wavy brunette hair with sideswept bangs. This reminded Annette of her own hairstyle, color and length when not on duty, though hers was usually parted in the middle, with chin-length bangs, and she preferred a looped updo while at work. "We'll need this picture and a general description of your daughter to work with."

"I understand," Maureen said. "Anything I can do to help bring Juliet home."

Just then, Detective Will Hossack lumbered into the office, after having gone to follow up on a suspected burglary. The thirty-eight-year-old full-time detective and ladies' man had been with the sheriff's department for fifteen years and seemed in no hurry to go elsewhere in law enforcement. Six-four and of solid build, he was dark-eyed, clean-shaven, and wore his brown hair in a Caesar cut underneath the Stetson hat atop his head. "Who do we have here?" he asked curiously.

"This is Maureen McCade," Annette told him. "Her daughter, Juliet McCade, has been missing since last night." Annette made eye contact with the detective warily. She could almost read his mind. Both victims of the Christmas Lights Killer had been missing, at least briefly, till their bodies were discovered. Would this case of a missing young woman also end tragically?

INDIANA STATE POLICE Senior Trooper Hamilton McCade cruised down the lightly snow-covered US Route 24 in his white Dodge Charger Pursuit in District 22, located in Fort Wayne, Allen County. He was on the lookout for anyone involved in criminal activity or violating the traffic laws. As standard practice, he was armed with a SIG Sauer P227 pistol as his primary weapon and had a SIG Sauer P365 subcompact pistol as a backup firearm, while wearing a ballistic vest. Though he had been at this for the past ten of his thirty-six years of life, moving from one ISP district to another while gaining some valuable experience and fulfillment, Hamilton thought it was time he moved up the ranks. Toward that end and in line with his recently completed PhD in criminal justice from Indiana University Bloomington, he had applied to join the ISP's Investigations Command Special Investigation Section. Or, more specifically, the Organized Crime and Corruption Unit within, believing this would better serve his goals of going after those who committed investment scams, trafficking offenses, political corruption and related offenses. There was every reason to believe that he would be reassigned accordingly early in the new year.

But for now, Hamilton was more focused on maintaining the status quo and trying to get through the holiday season all by his lonesome. Although dumped six months ago by his girlfriend, Felicity Sheridan, who seemed to believe the pastures were greener with the investment banker she'd met on an online dating app, Hamilton wouldn't exactly say he was ready to swear off women and romance forever. But it had shaken his confidence in that department, in spite of being a guy in pretty good shape at six-three, and certainly able to hold his own in the looks department, with his deep blue eyes and black hair in a short military-style cut. All he could do for the time being was wait and see if someone who struck his fancy came along, and go from there.

Hamilton drove down West Jefferson Boulevard and saw nothing out of the ordinary. He lowered the brim of his campaign hat, mainly out of habit, as his thoughts drifted to his only living family. His sister, Maureen, was six years older and still living in his hometown of Carol Creek in the adjacent Dabs County, where she was a registered nurse. They had drifted apart somewhat once he'd left for greater opportunities in Fort Wayne. But even that didn't stop him from appreciating how Maureen had always been in his corner when their parents, Sherman and Catherine McCade, had more or less left them to fend for themselves. When Maureen had made a mistake with a one-night stand resulting in pregnancy, with no accountability by the father, Hamilton had tried to step in there as much as possible for his sister and the beautiful girl she'd brought into this world. It was hard for him to believe that Juliet was now twenty-one years old and trying to make a life for herself. While reminding Hamilton of Maureen, Juliet resembled their mother more.

Maybe he would return home for Christmas this year and the three of them could spend it together and even ring in the new year as a family, before it was time for him to get back to the grind of the life he had established in Fort Wayne. When his cell phone rang, Hamilton snapped out of his reverie. He took the phone from the side pocket of the trousers worn with his uniform and glanced at it. *Wouldn't you know it*, he thought, grinning, when he saw that the caller was none other than Maureen.

Placing the phone in the car's cell phone holder, he tapped the speaker icon and said in a pleasant voice, "Hey, sis. I was just thinking about you and Juliet."

"Juliet's missing," Maureen said in a panicky voice.

"What do you mean she's missing?" Hamilton asked equably.

"I haven't seen her since last night. She was supposed to go out with a girlfriend, but never showed up. She texted me around seven forty to say she thought someone was following her, but didn't respond when I texted back. I hate to bother you with this, but I'm freaking out here, wondering if Juliet's in real trouble."

I hope she's okay, Hamilton thought, not wanting to jump the gun on this. "Have you reported her missing to the sheriff's department?" He knew that there was no timetable for filing reports of missing persons, but there was also no obligation to act upon it right away if there were other priorities. Particularly for a small office usually stretched thin.

"Yes, I talked to Detective Annette Lynley," Maureen said. "And later, Detective Will Hossack. They assured me this was being taken seriously, especially with a serial killer on the loose in Carol Creek."

"Let's hope so." Hamilton chewed on his lower lip musingly. He knew Hossack, having worked with him on a case or two over the years. Hadn't had the pleasure of meeting Annette Lynley. Presumably she was up to the job in locating Juliet. The thought that his niece could have become the victim of the so-called Christmas Lights Killer left Hamilton feeling numb. His dissertation had been on serial killers and the dynamics that drove them to commit multiple murders while instilling terror in their chosen communities. He wasn't prepared to go there, though, knowing full well from past experience that twenty-one-year-olds were prone to staying out all night long and well into the next day without regard to clearing it first with parents. Or even considering their feelings when making reckless and risky choices. He wasn't sure how Juliet fit into this equation, not being as tuned into her life as a young adult as perhaps he should have been. He had to believe that somehow this would end on a good note and Juliet would return home to her mother, safe and sound.

Maureen drew a breath. "I'm really worried about Juliet and what could have happened to her and just thought you should know."

"I'm glad you told me," Hamilton said, trying to remain positive. "I'll drop by the sheriff's office and see what the status is on their investigation."

"Would you?"

"Of course. Juliet is my niece and I want to know she's all right," he promised her.

Maureen heaved an audible sigh, obviously ill at ease.

"If she calls or shows up, let me know."

"I will."

After disconnecting, he headed toward the highway that would take him to Carol Creek. It would be about forty-five minutes to get there on snowy roads. Dabs County was one of the counties within the ISP District 22 jurisdiction, giving Hamilton the ability to travel there, in spite of making a detour from the area he normally patrolled.

When he reached the sheriff's department, Hamilton walked to the brick building, ignoring the cold air hitting him in the face like a slap. The moment he stepped inside, he spotted an attractive and slender biracial woman in her thirties, with pretty, brownish green eyes, a dainty nose and a nice, full mouth—all on a high-cheeked, oval face. Her obviously long brunette hair was in a businesslike updo. About five-seven, a perfect height to his own size, she was wearing a dark blue blazer with matching pants, a white shirt and ankle boots, and carried herself with confidence.

She met his eyes squarely and said with a smile, "Hi, I'm Detective Annette Lynley." She gave him and his uniform the once-over. "I'm guessing that you're with the ISP?"

"Indiana State Trooper Hamilton McCade," he confirmed.

Annette reacted to the name. "You wouldn't happen to be related to Juliet McCade?"

"Juliet's my niece." His mouth tightened as he remembered he needed to cut to the chase. "I want to know exactly what you're doing to locate Juliet, who I believe is still missing?"

Chapter Two

Annette studied the Indiana state trooper. Hamilton McCade was a good-looking man with a square face, profoundly blue eyes, aquiline nose, slanted mouth and a slightly jutting chin, clean-shaven. He was tall, she imagined around six-three, and filled out his trooper uniform nicely. She got only a glimpse of his dark hair in what appeared to be a military cut beneath his campaign hat. Suddenly realizing she was staring, Annette averted her eyes briefly before gazing at him again. "Why don't we step into my office, Trooper McCade," she said, fully appreciating his concern for his missing niece.

"Lead the way, Detective," he said stiffly.

Before they could get there, Will Hossack stepped from his own office and the two men eyed each other. "Thought I recognized the voice," Will said amiably. "What's up, Hamilton? Been a minute."

"Hey, Will." He shook the large hand that the slightly taller Will put before him.

Annette raised a brow. "You two know each other?"

"Our paths have crossed on occasion during investigations," Will explained. "And we might have gone out for a drink or two to talk shop," he added mischievously.

"I see." She almost felt like the odd one out, but knew realistically that with both of them both having been in law enforcement in the area longer than she had, it wasn't too surprising that they would be acquainted.

"So, what brings you our way, Trooper Mc-Cade?" Will asked curiously in a more formal manner.

"As I was telling Detective Lynley," Hamilton replied, "I'm here to check on your efforts to find my missing niece, Juliet."

"Wait a sec." Will's head snapped back. "Juliet McCade's your niece?"

"Yeah."

"Never made the connection," Will said apologetically.

"Wouldn't have expected you to," Hamilton muttered. "I understand that my sister, Maureen McCade, was here earlier?"

"Right." Will looked down at his water-resistant boots and back at him. "Detective Lynley took your sister's statement and she can bring you up to date on where things stand."

Hamilton faced her and Annette actually felt a tiny quiver from the intensity of his blue eyes. "Why don't we get to it then."

Annette nodded and glanced at Will, who seemed to silently wish her good luck. Before heading back to his own office, Will told Hamilton, "I know the tendency in these instances is to think the worst, but I'm sure your niece will turn up fine."

"I want to believe that," Hamilton said. "Until it happens, though, I need to be able to reassure my sister that this is not being pushed to the back burners."

"It's not," Annette promised him. What she couldn't bring herself to say, just yet, was that it worried her that Juliet had vanished at a time when a serial killer was on the prowl. And that the longer Hamilton's niece remained unaccounted for, the greater the likelihood that this might not come to a happy conclusion.

HAMILTON SAT IN the barrel chair on the opposite side of the gorgeous detective's desk. He couldn't help but wonder if she was married. Was she dating? Did she have children? Or was she single, childless and available, like him? He wasn't counting on the latter, figuring it was probably a long shot for the thirtysomething detective to have hung around in her life just waiting for him to appear. Even that was being premature, since they weren't exactly meeting for dating purposes, much less getting past that point to things more intimate and interesting. No, right now, he needed to stay focused on finding his niece so his sister could put her worries about Juliet to rest.

As though reading his mind, Annette said in a serious tone, "First, you should know, Trooper McCade, that we're doing everything we can to locate your niece."

He was certainly happy to hear that, for a start, and said, "Why don't you call me Hamilton, Detective Lynley."

"All right," she agreed. "In turn, you can call me Annette."

"Annette it is." He liked the name that somehow suited her. "Tell me more…"

She paused. "Since you're in law enforcement yourself, I'm sure you know that in most instances of missing persons, where there's no evidence of clear and present danger or foul play, we usually wait at least twenty-four hours before launching an investigation in earnest."

Hamilton understood this all too well and for good reason. He had certainly done his fair share of participating in cases involving missing persons. More than half a million persons were reported missing in the United States annually. The vast majority proved to be alive and well, returning home within twenty-four hours. He got that and found the data encouraging. But there was still that elephant in the room—a serial killer in town—which undermined those usually favorable odds for a young woman's safe return. "In this instance, waiting a day is too long," he argued knowingly, sure that she got his meaning. "The sooner you can locate Juliet, the better."

"I agree," Annette said coolly. "Toward that end, we've put out a BOLO alert for Juliet and her Subaru Impreza."

"That's good," he said, fearing the possibility that Juliet could have been in an accident and was therefore unresponsive.

"We're also using cell tower triangulation to see if we can pinpoint where Juliet last used her phone, whether it was the text message sent to Maureen or otherwise."

Hamilton nodded approvingly. "That can help."

Annette leaned forward. "We're also checking with hospitals for anyone fitting her description, if the patient is unnamed."

Hamilton flinched at the thought of Juliet being hospitalized as a Jane Doe, with her identification missing and Maureen not there by her side. "Okay," he muttered.

"If Juliet isn't found inside of twenty-four hours, we're prepared to organize search teams of volunteers to accompany law enforcement's efforts," Annette informed him. "Beyond that, if need be, we'll notify the FBI, its National Center for the Analysis of Violent Behavior and the Violent Criminal Apprehension Program within, your department officially, the National Missing and Unidentified Persons System, and, of course, the Indiana Clearinghouse for Information on Missing Children and Missing Endangered Adults."

Hamilton was admittedly impressed that the detective seemed to have all the bases covered in giving them their best shot at locating Juliet. He just wondered if it would be enough. "Well, I thank you for your current and future efforts, Annette."

"It's my job, Hamilton," she stressed. "With any luck, your niece simply lost her bearings, as young people tend to do these days, and will be totally embarrassed about it when she gets home and tries to explain."

He grinned, picturing the scenario, while knowing that as an only child, Juliet had perfected over the years the art of getting back into her mother's good graces after having gone off the rails a bit. Were that the case this time around, too, he was sure that Maureen would be completely forgiving again, although having been scared half to death by her daughter, and they would get on with any plans for Christmas.

Though he almost found himself hating to leave the detective's office, Hamilton knew it was time he did just that. "I won't take up any more of your time," he said, getting to his feet.

Annette stood, too, offering him a smile. "I understand how stressful something like this can be, especially at this time of year. If you want to give me your number, I can keep you informed on where this goes."

Hamilton gave her his cell phone number and was given hers in return, which he added to his contacts.

"As soon as we hear anything concrete," she said, "I'll let you know."

"Thanks." He met her eyes and realized that she had extended a hand. Shaking it, Hamilton noticed how soft her skin felt against his. He couldn't help but imagine that this softness was likely present from her face down to her feet and everywhere in between. The thought caused a stir in him. He released her surprisingly firm grip and showed himself out. Even as he walked away, he sensed her watching him.

After getting back in his vehicle, Hamilton called his sister. "Hey. Any word from Juliet?"

"No, not yet," Maureen said dolefully.

"I just left the sheriff's office," he told her. "They're pulling out all the stops to try and find her." He imagined Juliet being held against her will somewhere, unable to communicate. As bad as that was, it was preferable to what happened to those women killed by the serial killer.

"We'll just pray that they succeed," his sister said. "Or that Juliet finds her way home all on her own."

"Yeah." He took a breath. "Look, I have to go back to work. If she comes home or you hear from her…"

"You'll be the first one I call," Maureen promised.

After disconnecting, Hamilton started up the Dodge Charger Pursuit and got on the road. He thought about Annette Lynley. Even after Juliet's case was settled, hopefully with a positive outcome, he felt he wanted to see the detective again. Maybe get to know her better, if she was open to that. If not, it was still a nice thought.

WHEN ANNETTE LEFT the sheriff's office for home, there had still been no sign of Juliet McCade, now nearly twenty-four hours after her disappearance. *Where are you?* Annette asked in her head as she drove her department-issued white Chrysler 300 Touring L down Cherry-wood Street. With no sign of the missing woman's car, Annette wondered if Juliet might have driven off somewhere, with or without someone accompanying her. If so, did she do it under force? Or simply to get away from her troubles, if she had any?

Annette's greater fears were that Juliet had run into harm's way, with no getting out of it alive. But until there was confirmation of this, they had to assume that she was still alive. Annette thought about Hamilton McCade. As a state trooper, he had obviously seen his share of misfortunes. But none hurt like those too close to home. Losing her adopted parents in a car accident a few years ago had devastated Annette. She'd never even gotten a chance to say good-bye to them and thank them again for bringing her into their lives. Having her siblings to lean on allowed her to get through it and carry on.

She sensed a strong bond existed between Hamilton and his sister as well. He must be close to his niece, too. Annette wondered if he had any children. A wife? Was he seeing anyone? Or was his whole life wrapped around his work in law enforcement, which sometimes seemed to be the story of her life. *Maybe it's none of my business*, she mused, turning down Wesmire

Lane. The fact that the handsome trooper had entered her world unintentionally and with more important things on his mind than romancing a fellow officer of the law hardly meant he was available and interested. She would do well to keep her eye on the ball. Especially after the disaster her last relationship had turned out to be.

Annette pulled into the driveway of her two-story home on a dead-end street. While the other homes nearby were illuminated outside with Christmas lights, she had opted against putting up decorations inside or out this year. Not that she had anything against celebrating Christmas. Just the opposite. It was her favorite time of the year. But maybe not this year, with the uptick in homicides, thanks in large part to a serial murderer at large. Then there was the current case of a missing twenty-one-year-old to dampen the holiday spirit.

Making footprints in the snow, Annette stepped onto the porch and unlocked the door before heading inside the country-style house that was surrounded by mature red maple trees. She turned on the lights near the foyer and took in the place that had been brand-new when she moved in nearly a year ago. It had an open concept with a spacious living-dining area and a gourmet kitchen, triple-pane windows, cathedral ceiling, and prefinished hickory hardwood flooring throughout. She had put in a combination of modern and rustic furniture and liked the way everything was arranged.

Heading into the kitchen, Annette turned on the kettle and got out a packet of instant hot cocoa. Once the drink was ready, she took her steaming ceramic mug and went back into the living room. She wondered if maybe her house should have some decorations for the holiday. Again, she pushed back at the notion. Apart from her workload, it might be too much to go through with only her to appreciate. Then there was the fact that she planned to celebrate Christmas day in Oklahoma this year with her siblings, in the sprawling house their parents had left them. After debating whether or not to sell it when they died, the Lynley siblings had decided that they would keep the property as a place to meet up or a vacation spot for anyone who wished to stay there.

Annette wondered if she would need to change her plans for Christmas, wincing at the thought of the nonrefundable round-trip ticket she'd purchased to Oklahoma City. She loved the opportunity for everyone to gather in one place but, admittedly, she wasn't in the best holiday spirit at the moment. She wasn't sure how appropriate it would be to leave Carol Creek and its citizens if a serial killer was still running amok. But there was still time to make an arrest and end the terror.

She sat on a corner of the leather square-arm sofa and sipped the cocoa before setting it on the coffee table. She then grabbed her laptop for a video chat with her brother Russell. With just a few months between them, she was closest in age to him among her siblings. But she hadn't been able to catch up much with him of late, now that Russell, an FBI special agent, was a married man again, having wed Rosamund Santiago, a Homeland Security Investigations special agent, last summer. Truthfully, Annette couldn't be happier for the newlyweds, both of whom had experienced tragedies in their lives. She only hoped she could be so lucky as to find true love with the right guy someday.

"Hey," she said when Russell's handsome face, bordered by raven locks in a high, tight haircut, appeared on the screen.

He gazed back at her with crinkled, steel gray eyes. "Hey, sis."

"How are things your way?"

"All good," he told her. "Busy at work, enjoying married life and all that."

"Nice to hear." She thought sadly about him losing his first wife and daughter in a home invasion.

"So, what's happening in your neck of the woods?" he asked instinctively.

"It's crazy around here right now," Annette confessed.

His chin jutted. "How crazy?"

"Since you asked, a serial killer is on the loose and a woman is missing."

Russell's brows knitted. "You think the two are connected?"

"I'm hoping that isn't the case, but I'm starting to worry since she's been missing for a day now."

"Let's not assume the worst, Annette," he said delicately. "These things don't always end badly. Often, it's just the opposite."

"I know," she conceded. "Still, the clock's ticking."

"Assuming the Bureau isn't already on the case, if you want, I can make a call to the FBI field office in Indianapolis and see what they can do to assist."

"Thanks, but we're working it as best as possible at the moment while conferring with other local law enforcement agencies to see if they have similar homicide or missing person cases." She wasn't quite ready to say they were overwhelmed as a small sheriff's office, but they appeared to be headed in that direction.

"Okay. But if there's anything I can to do help, just ask."

"I will," she said, feeling better just talking to him. The conversation shifted to the Christmas gathering. "I'll do my best to make it," Annette promised, knowing that fell flat.

"Do better than that," Russell insisted. "As we both know all too well, life is too short to put it off to next year or later. I think we all need this."

"You're right, we do." She flashed her teeth at him. "I'll be there. Wouldn't miss it."

He grinned. "That's what I'm talking about."

"Say hello to Rosamund for me," Annette finished and Russell agreed, before they disconnected.

After dining on leftover lemon chicken and baked beans, Annette took a hot bath and called it an early night, wondering what tomorrow would bring.

She got her answer when she was awakened by the buzzing of her cell phone the next morning. The caller was Detective Will Hossack. "Will…" Annette tried to keep the sleepiness from her voice as she sat up uneasily in the canopy bed surrounded by traditional furnishings.

"We've located Juliet McCade's vehicle," he said tonelessly. "It was halfway in a ditch off Murdon Street, near the DeLuca Christmas Tree Farm."

Annette tensed. "And Juliet…?"

"No sign of her yet." He paused. "But there's a piece of clothing sticking out of the car's trunk."

"I'm on my way," she said succinctly, and ended the conversation. She feared the worst as she got off the bed. She changed out of her notch-collar pink pajamas and got dressed quickly, grabbed a bagel on the way out the door and headed for the location.

Chapter Three

When she arrived at the scene, Annette was greeted by Will, who, beneath his hat, had a dour look. Face reddened from the cold, he said grimly, "There was a body in the trunk. Deceased."

Her heart sank as Annette gazed at the front of the vehicle from her vantage point. She could see that the trunk was open. Eyeing the detective, she asked warily, "Who?"

"Appears to be the missing woman," Will responded. "Juliet McCade."

As the lead detective on the case, Annette knew she needed to see for herself, even if this was one of the most painful parts of the process. Along with notifying the next of kin. She glanced at a squad car with its flashing lights. Two tall and thickly built deputies stood beside it, conferring with each other. Annette headed toward the back of the Subaru Impreza. In the trunk was the fully clothed body of a young biracial female. Her disheveled brunette hair was long and wavy and had side-swept bangs. Wrapped around her neck was a string of Christmas lights. Annette recognized the decedent from the cell phone picture Maureen McCade had sent. Dead in the trunk was her daughter, Juliet McCade. Who was also the niece of Trooper Hamilton McCade.

"It's Juliet." Annette sucked in a deep breath, knowing her worst fears had been realized. "Just what we didn't need, and at this time," she muttered, wearing leather gloves to keep her hands warm.

"Yeah. You're right." Will wrinkled his nose. "Unfortunately, we got it anyway. Someone saw to that."

"Hmm…" She walked over to the driver's side of the vehicle and looked inside through the window. There was nothing that caught her eye at a glance.

"The car was unlocked," Will pointed out. "The victim's handbag, cell phone and any identification seem to be missing, though it's likely we'll find them strewn about and buried beneath the overnight snowfall."

"That's a good possibility," Annette concurred, knowing this had been the pattern of the unsub, who seemed mostly interested in buying time in having them identify his victims by scattering their identifying documents and cell phone. Perhaps to put greater distance between him and them, figuratively and literally. "Who discovered the car?" she wondered aloud, knowing that they had assembled search teams to comb the wooded and rural areas of the county after twenty-four hours had passed without word from Juliet McCade.

"Deputies Andy Stackhouse and Michael Jorgenson over there spotted the vehicle while on routine patrol and, after running the plates, realized it belonged to the missing woman and called it in."

Annette glanced at the deputies and back. "Did they happen to see anyone coming or going from the scene?"

"No." Will rubbed his gloved hands together. "Judging by the snow on the car, I'm guessing it's been stuck in this ditch for hours. Whoever left it here had plenty of time to get away."

"I gathered as much." She was not at all surprised, considering the length of time since Juliet had been reported missing.

Annette wondered if the fresh snow covering the ground had all but eliminated any chance to follow up on tire or foot tracks. Still, she was hopeful that evidence might have been left behind here or there to be recovered by crime scene technicians and the medical examiner in an autopsy.

Before Annette could digest the tragedy further, the coroner's van pulled up. Getting out was the Dabs County coroner and medical examiner, Dr. Josephine Washburn. In her late forties, the slim woman had a short bob in a gray ombré color and blue eyes. "Got here as soon as I could," she said, gazing at Annette.

"Sorry you had to come at all," Annette muttered, knowing the bleak nature of any such visit.

Josephine shrugged. "I could say the same for you, Detective. Unfortunately for both of us, it comes with the territory. So, where is she?"

"Right this way," Will told her, leading her to the back of the car.

The ME frowned as she looked in the trunk. "Not a very nice way to have your life ended."

"I was thinking the same thing," Annette said. She wondered how long it took the victim to lose consciousness and end her misery.

Josephine put on latex gloves as she did her preliminary examination of the dead woman. After a few minutes, she said somberly, "My initial assessment is that the cause of death was ligature strangulation. And, as such, the deceased was a victim of homicide."

"We figured as much, given the string lights

around her neck," Annette said sadly, glancing at Will and back.

Josephine twisted her lips. "It looks like the Christmas Lights Killer has struck again."

"So it would seem," Annette had to agree, while wondering how to break this devastating news to Hamilton. As well as to his sister. "What's your estimate on the time of death?"

The coroner considered this while regarding the victim. "Based on her appearance and other factors, I estimate that she's been dead for maybe a day and a half or so. If that calculation changes, I'll let you know."

"All right." Annette thought about the time Juliet had sent the text message to Maureen. Seven forty that night. The estimation of when Juliet died would indicate that she was likely killed shortly after indicating to her mom that someone was following her. Had this been why she'd ended up in a ditch? Trying to get away from a stalker who'd been driving, as opposed to one on foot?

When the crime scene technicians arrived, they went about processing the scene and taking photographs, including of the victim, before Juliet was placed in the coroner's van and transported to the Dabs County Morgue.

While Annette was going over what they knew and didn't know, crime scene analyst Loretta Covington approached them. "I think I may have found something…"

Annette eyed the short CSA, who was in her thirties, with brown eyes and brown hair in a cropped pixie. She wore protective clothing. "What is it?" Annette asked.

"A tire track," Loretta replied. "Just down there a bit. We think it could have come from another vehicle that might have forced the Subaru Impreza off the road."

"Show us," Will told her.

"Sure thing."

They followed her about thirty feet on the same side of the street that Juliet would have been driving on. Annette took a look at the tire track, which was beneath a clump of bushes, preventing it from being covered over by snow. If this had been made by the driver of another vehicle in pursuit of Juliet's car, the unsub might have temporarily lost control of the vehicle before correcting. Or the tire track could be totally unrelated to Juliet's death.

"You may be on to something," she told the CSA hopefully. "It's worth a try."

"Yeah," Will agreed. "Let's see if we can find out who left the track and take it from there."

"Will do," Loretta promised, and assembled other CSAs to make a cast of the tire track.

Annette knew they would need to look for

possible witnesses and gather information about Juliet's acquaintances, her two jobs, and comings and goings. But first things first. There needed to be a positive identification of the deceased, something that Annette wasn't particularly looking forward to as Hamilton McCade entered her head.

HAMILTON HAD BARELY gotten a wink of sleep last night, his mind too active in worry about his niece. No matter how she acted at times as if she was invincible, like a typical twenty-one-year-old, or how much she proved to be a handful for a sometimes overprotective mother, this was not like Juliet. She wouldn't simply leave Maureen hanging for over a day now.

At least that's not my impression of her, he thought as he drove down US Route 30. Something had to be very wrong. After leaving the sheriff's office last night, he had driven around for more than an hour searching for Juliet's car, hoping to find her stuck somewhere, but other than that alive and well. If not cold and frustrated. But he hadn't spotted her or the Subaru anywhere. So, where was she? Had Juliet driven away from the immediate area of her own accord? If so, would she contact Maureen today and ease her concerns?

It would make me feel a lot better, too, Hamilton told himself as he continued driving his duty vehicle, looking for any signs of trouble on the streets. Best to look at the glass half-full than half-empty, he believed. Otherwise, this would probably drive him crazy. He had considered taking the day off to join in the official search for Juliet. But he'd decided to let the sheriff's department do their job without his interference. At least for the short-term. Annette Lynley, in particular, certainly seemed more than up to the task of conducting a missing person investigation. And Will Hossack was a good detective who would do his part as well in trying to locate Juliet, whatever it took.

If they haven't made any progress by the time I take my lunch break, I'll swing back over to Carol Creek and look for Juliet again myself, Hamilton told himself. As he drove down the highway, he spotted in front of him a black Dodge Challenger SRT Hellcat Redeye. The first thing that caught his eye was that the temporary license plate was incorrectly located on the back window. Then there was the fact that the male driver seemed overly cautious in being slightly under the speed limit. Hamilton admitted to himself that the latter may have been a defensive move once the driver realized he was tailing him, as was often the case when drivers became aware of ISP troopers in the vicinity. He may have simply let this one slide, but Hamilton sensed that he should check it out, and give himself something else to think about other than his missing niece.

He motioned to the driver to pull over to the side of the road and, after seemingly weighing his options, the driver complied. Hamilton pulled up behind him, hoping this would be routine and not turn into anything serious. He exited his vehicle and approached the driver's side of the Dodge Challenger. The man inside, whom Hamilton judged to be in his early thirties, had already lowered the window.

"Did I do something wrong, Officer?" he asked in a calm voice.

Hamilton perused him quickly. He was slender and triangular-faced, with messy black hair cut short on the sides. He had blue eyes that looked clear and a chinstrap beard, same color as his hair. Hamilton glanced further into the vehicle and saw a brown paper bag on the passenger seat. "What's in the bag?" he asked suspiciously, thinking it might be a firearm. As such, Hamilton kept his guard up and was ready to access his SIG Sauer P227 pistol in a hurry, if need be.

"Just a ham and cheese sandwich," the man answered coolly. "I can show you, if you want?"

"Do it." Hamilton deepened his voice. "If it's

a weapon, I promise you I'm quicker than you are." He watched the man like a hawk while sliding a hand on the firearm in his duty holster. When the man pulled the sandwich out of the bag and showed it was empty, Hamilton relaxed, lifting his hand off the weapon. "What's your name, sir?" he asked the driver politely.

"Mack Cardwell," the man answered.

"Mr. Cardwell, the interim license plate of your new vehicle is in the wrong spot on the back window."

"Really?" Cardwell cocked a brow. "Sorry about that. Where is it supposed to be?"

"Actually, the temporary plate should be affixed to the window on the left side while facing the rear of the vehicle," Hamilton informed him.

"No problem, Officer. I can take care of that right away."

"You do that." Hamilton met his gaze and somehow felt uncomfortable with it. Was he hiding something? "Can you show me your driver's license, Mr. Cardwell?"

"Sure," he agreed. "Happy to cooperate." He removed a wallet from the pocket of his jeans, took out the license and handed it over.

Hamilton studied the license. Mack Anthony Cardwell. The date of birth put him at thirty-two years of age, three months shy of thirty-three. He lived in Dabs County in the town of

Laraville on Wailby Crest Lane. Homing in on the photograph and back at the driver, Hamilton believed they were one and the same. Still, there was an uneasiness that gnawed at his insides regarding the man. "Are you in any trouble, Mr. Cardwell?"

"No, sir," he insisted with a straight face. "I'm clean."

We'll see about that, Hamilton thought. "Give me a minute to check on that. Stay put."

"I'm not going anywhere," he promised.

Hamilton went back to his vehicle and ran the name for any outstanding arrest warrants or criminal record. Both came back negative. *Looks like Cardwell's good as his word*, Hamilton told himself, and went back to the driver.

"Any problems?" the man asked, as though confident in the answer.

"None." Hamilton handed the driver's license back and issued him a citation for incorrectly placing the interim license plate. "You're free to go."

"Thanks." Cardwell grinned sideways. "I'll be sure to put the temp license plate where it's supposed to be."

"Good." Hamilton softened the hardness of his stare. "Enjoy the rest of your day."

"I'll try," he said. "Thanks."

Once back inside his car, Hamilton waited

till Mack Anthony Cardwell drove off, before hitting the road again himself. He'd barely had time to assess whether his instincts were right or way off about the man, when his cell phone rang. He slid it out of the pocket of his uniform's winter jacket and saw that the caller was Detective Annette Lynley.

"Trooper McCade," he answered, as if speaking to a total stranger.

"Trooper… Hamilton," Annette stammered. "Your niece's vehicle has been located."

"Oh…?" That gave him hope. Except that the detective's tone sounded like the news got worse, not better.

"A body was found in the trunk." Annette sighed. "We have reason to believe that it is Juliet McCade. I'm afraid she's dead." Another pause. "She was the victim of a ligature strangulation. I'm so sorry for your loss …"

Hamilton muttered an expletive to himself. How could this happen? Who was responsible? Obviously, Juliet didn't put herself in the trunk of her own car. Was this the work of a serial killer? Or someone else who had come after her? Hamilton thought about his sister and how worried she must be in not hearing from Juliet. "Have you told Maureen yet?"

"Actually, I'm about to head over to her house

right now," Annette informed him. "I thought she needed to hear this face-to-face."

"I'd like to be there when you tell her," he said with a jagged edge to his voice. If he couldn't have come to the rescue of his niece, the least Hamilton wanted to do was be there for his sister in her moment of need.

"I understand," Annette said softly. "I can meet you at her place."

When he disconnected, a wave of emotions surged through Hamilton. From shock to sorrow to anger and everything in between. But mostly he wanted justice for Juliet, whose death had come way too soon, all but ensuring that maintaining the holiday spirit would be difficult. If not impossible.

ANNETTE WAITED IN her car outside the midcentury modern two-story home on Mulligan Road. It was decorated with Christmas lights. A silver Honda Odyssey was parked in the driveway. Though she had done this before, it never got any easier to have to tell a mother, father, brother, sister, or even an uncle, that a loved one had passed away. And yet this was how it was done. Unfortunately, it happened all too often in society these days. Worse in this case was, judging by the MO and pending the autopsy report, the likelihood that the victim had been murdered by a serial killer. If so, it could mean that Juliet had been targeted, though she could have been just as easily randomly selected to go after.

Annette watched as Hamilton's Dodge Charger Pursuit pulled up behind her. Hard as it would be, she welcomed his company in having to break the terrible news to his sister. Maureen would need her brother to help her get through this ordeal. Annette got out of her car and met him in front of the house. "I know how difficult this must be for you," she stated sadly.

"Yeah, I'm still processing it," he admitted, touching the brim of his hat. "Just tell me, was the so-called Christmas Lights Killer responsible for this?"

"It looks that way." She paused. "We'll have a better read on that once the autopsy has been completed, along with assessing and processing the crime scene evidence, or lack thereof."

He frowned thoughtfully. "You never expect this to happen to someone in the family."

"I know." Annette considered the violent end to the lives of her brother's first wife and daughter. "But then, it's always someone's family, right?"

"Yeah, so true." Hamilton sucked in a deep breath. "Let's just get this over with."

She nodded, while knowing it would never be

over with till the unsub was taken into custody
and held accountable for his crimes. She followed Hamilton up the walkway. The front door
of the house opened the moment they scaled
the three concrete steps to the porch. Maureen
stood there, her face anguished, like a mother
who was able to read the dire writing on the
wall. Her eyes darted from Annette to Hamilton, and back again. "Juliet's dead, isn't she?"

Before Annette could respond, Hamilton put
his large hands on his sister's shoulders and said
tenderly, "Why don't we go inside?"

Maureen refused to budge, blocking the en-
tryway. "Just tell me!" she demanded. "Have
you found my daughter alive and well? Or not?"

Guessing that Hamilton couldn't bring himself to tell her what she needed to hear, Annette
did her job. "I'm sorry to have to tell you that
your daughter is dead. Her body was found in
the trunk of her car."

Maureen seemed to lose it in that moment.
Her legs became unsteady and Hamilton
stopped her from falling, guiding her into the
house. Annette followed, whereupon she immediately laid eyes on a tall, eastern white pine in
a corner of the living room, fully decorated for
Christmas, with several wrapped gifts beneath
it. She took her eyes away and had a cursory
glance of other decorations and the contempo-

rary furnishings on plush brown carpeting, before turning back to Maureen, who was being embraced by Hamilton.

"We'll get through this," he said, trying to comfort his sister.

Maureen pulled away from him and glared at Annette. "Do you know who killed her?"

"We're still investigating it," she said, not wanting to jump the gun.

Maureen favored Hamilton with a bleak stare. "My only child is dead. How do I live with that?"

He sighed raggedly. "By staying strong," he said matter-of-factly. "It's what Juliet would have wanted. We both need to come to grips with this and let the authorities get to the bottom of it."

Maureen nodded as she wiped away tears from her eyes. Though hating to further intrude upon her grief, Annette was still duty bound to tell the victim's next of kin what needed to be done now. "You'll have to come to the morgue to identify the body," she said gently.

Hamilton regarded Annette hotly. "I'll do it."

She had expected as much from him, as the decedent's uncle and a state trooper who had likely dealt with death in his line of work. "Okay."

Annette was sympathetic enough to allow

them to take the time needed to deal with their emotions before Hamilton positively ID'd the body. She also knew this was her time to leave them alone to commiserate, while wishing there was more to say or do. But there was never enough on either front. All she could do now was ensure that justice was done for Juliet McCade.

HE COULDN'T HAVE asked for a better victim. She was young and pretty. Gullible and afraid. Simple and not so simple. Ready to die. Yet fighting to stay alive till there was no more fight in her. It was the same way with the other victims. He caught them in a vulnerable state and before they could realize what he had in mind, it was much too late to do anything about it. Other than see their lives flash before their eyes in a final moment of reflection before it all faded to black.

Strangling the latest one with the Christmas string lights had given him a rush of adrenaline that zipped throughout his body. Stuffing her dead body in the trunk of her car was a spontaneous move on his part to throw the authorities off balance while he made a clean getaway. With Christmas just two weeks away, there was still work to be done. Others would die and he would exact more vengeance on the one who'd gotten away.

He drove around town, knowing it was a new day and that there was sure to be more investigating by the cops now that the body had been discovered. They would be doing everything they could to stop him. Well, have at it. He was cleverer than them. Not to mention, much more ruthless and determined to carry out the killings in Carol Creek, ensuring that the Christmas season would be soiled by the specter of death and terror, with him leading the way joyously.

He gripped the steering wheel hard while visions of strangling his chosen ones danced in his head. Soon, another would have the life drained out of her and his Christmas wishes would continue to come true, with an imagined big red bow on top of his pretty presents.

Chapter Four

Hamilton needed just one brief look at the decedent to know it was his niece. Juliet was on a shelf in the morgue refrigerator. He saw only her face, which had lost some of its complexion in death, her eyes closed as though she were asleep. It was framed by tangled, long and wavy brunette hair with the bangs swept to the sides. Just to be doubly sure, he asked for the shelf to be pulled out a bit more. The lanky male morgue attendant, a thirtysomething with curly two-tone hair, complied, and Hamilton checked Juliet's right shoulder. There it was, the butterfly tattoo, telling him he was indeed looking at his sister's only child.

"It's her," he confirmed morosely.

He turned away from the corpse and Annette told the attendant, "We're done." Juliet was returned to the cabinet, where Hamilton knew she would remain till the autopsy. The thought of his niece being put through the process was difficult, but he understood it was a necessary procedure for anyone dying under unnatural or suspicious circumstances. That didn't make it any less unsettling for him. "Sorry you had to go through that," Annette said once they were outside.

"So am I, but it had to be done," Hamilton stated. "I'd rather it be me to identify the body than Maureen."

"I understand." Annette took a breath. "I want you to know that the sheriff's office will do everything in its power to find out who killed your niece and make sure the unsub is held accountable."

Hamilton's lips curled at the corner. "Is that what you told the loved ones of the other victims of a serial killer?" he questioned. "Doesn't seem to be working out very well, does it? How many more women will have to die before this creep is arrested?"

"You have every right to be frustrated," she responded in a calm voice. "No one wanted to see any of the women murdered. Least of all me. But as cliché as it sounds, these things do occur sometimes, even in small towns like Carol Creek. Yes, there's a psychopath out there. And he's chosen to kill during the Christmas season. As the lead detective on the case, with Will Hossack working alongside me, I can tell you neither of us has any intention of letting up till we catch this guy. Whatever it takes," Annette indicated sharply.

Hamilton realized he had been wholly unfair to her and the sheriff's department. They were no more at fault than he was that Juliet happened to have gotten into the crosshairs of a killer. Few homicide cases were solved overnight, no matter the culprit. This was obviously truer when the killer was making a conscious and carefully orchestrated effort to avoid capture.

"Sorry for venting," Hamilton apologized to the detective whom he wanted as an ally and not adversary. "I know you're doing your job in every case that comes your way."

"Apology accepted." Annette gazed at him compassionately. "I need to get back to the investigation, but promise to keep you in the loop."

"Okay." He wanted more than to be kept in the loop so long as Juliet's killer remained free. But now was not the time to be confrontational again. "I'd better go check on Maureen." His sister needed him more now than ever, if she was to get past this and come out whole on the other side. And even that was no sure thing.

Annette nodded understandingly. "We'll get the perp, one way or the other."

Hamilton felt her conviction and hoped they would be able to work together toward a common goal. Beyond that, there was the reality of needing to bury his niece and deal with the aftermath.

When he got back to his sister's house, it pained Hamilton to have to confirm what she had already resigned herself to. It still needed to be said. "Juliet is gone," he said in affirmation. "I'm so sorry, Maureen." As she started to weep, he wrapped her in his arms. "We'll get through this," he promised, while wondering just how long that would take. The fact that his niece was never coming back would likely haunt them for the rest of their lives.

"What did Juliet ever do to deserve this?" Maureen cried into his shoulder.

"Not a damned thing." Hamilton took a deep breath. "No one deserves to be murdered. Least of all a twenty-one-year-old with her entire life ahead of her. This wasn't in any way, shape or form Juliet's fault," he stressed. "She simply happened to be in the wrong place at the wrong time." He understood that this did little to take away the blunt reality of losing someone to violence, but hoped it gave some context nonetheless.

Maureen pulled away from him. "You should go back to work."

"I'm not going to leave you," he told her.

"I need to be alone," she insisted. "To process this."

Hamilton wanted to push back against that, feeling that family needed to be together at a time like this. And as they were only left with each other, that made it all the more important. But as everybody needed to grieve in their own way, he had to respect her decision. "All right," he relented. "I'll go. If you need me…"

"I'll be fine," she tried to say with a straight face. "I have to make some calls and arrangements to bury my daughter."

Her words tore through Hamilton as he was also left to have to say goodbye to his niece. Just as important to him was seeing to it that her death did not go unpunished. The sheriff's department would need to step up and solve this case. Which meant they would need to put a stop to a serial killer, one way or the other. Hamilton owed it to his sister and niece to do his part toward that end, whatever that entailed.

ANNETTE WAS AT her desk that afternoon when she was emailed a copy of Juliet McCade's autopsy report. She held her breath as she opened it and read. According to the report, the cause of death was ligature strangulation, with the manner of death listed as homicide. The weapon used to kill the victim was a string of Christmas lights, resulting in cerebral hypoxia, decreasing the brain's oxygen supply by compressing the blood vessels that fed it. Apart from the deep ligature marks found around Juliet's throat, there was some bruising on her arms, face and legs that the medical examiner believed was due to her struggling against her attacker and trying to stay alive.

Annette exhaled as she felt the same pain of loss and indignation that she had with the first two women who'd died this month in the same manner. But this time, she seemed to feel it more somehow, after the connection of sorts she'd made with Juliet's uncle, Hamilton Mc-Cade. Annette could only hope that he and his sister could come to terms with the death and find a way to cope. Meanwhile, a cold-blooded murderer was at large in Carol Creek and making a bold statement that he remained free to terrorize the community and there was no stopping him.

One other thing that caught her attention as she read through the rest of the report was the mention of a hair that was removed from Juliet's mouth. It did not match her own hair, indicating that it may have come from her attacker. Annette saw this as a solid lead toward catching the unsub.

When her cell phone rang a few minutes later, she lifted it from her desk and saw that it was the medical examiner, Josephine Washburn. "Hello."

"Just wanted to see if you received the autopsy report and had a chance to take a look at it."

"Yes and yes," Annette told her.

"I also sent it to Detective Hossack and Sheriff Teixeira," Josephine informed her routinely. "Any questions for me?"

"I wondered about the hair you took from the victim's mouth. What else can you tell me about it?"

"It definitely didn't belong to the decedent. The color was either dark brown or black and a different texture than the victim's hair. Can't say whether or not it belonged to the perpetrator. In accordance with potential evidence in a homicide, I have sent the hair to the Indiana State Police crime laboratory for further analysis."

That was standard procedure for local crimes, as the sheriff's office did not have its own crime lab. "Any other DNA collected?" she asked.

The ME indicated that there had been, but none that held the same potential weight of the strand of hair in terms of identifying who it belonged to. Josephine also said Juliet's body would soon be released for funeral arrangements, hoping to spare the victim's family as much pain as possible.

After the conversation, Annette left her office and stopped by Patti Gellar, the office clerk. "How're the twins?" she asked the fortysomething mother of Mia and Nikki.

"They're growing up way too fast," Patti complained, holding a steaming mug of coffee she was about to deliver to the sheriff.

Annette smiled, gazing at the slender, blue-eyed woman with brown hair in an A-line cut. "That's usually the case," she joked.

"Someday you'll get to experience the joy firsthand," Patti promised.

"Hope so." Annette looked forward to such a time in her life, while knowing that any such progeny would have more love than they knew what to do with. She headed to Will's office, a carbon copy of her own, only with contemporary furnishings that seemed to be more worn. He was standing by his desk when she stepped inside. "Did you read the autopsy report?" she asked.

"Yeah, just had a look." His brow furrowed. "Same old, same old. Sickening."

"There was something new," she pointed out. "The hair removed from the victim's mouth."

"True. Gives us something real to work with."

"Along with the tire track that may belong to the unsub's vehicle."

"That, too," he agreed.

"I'm on my way to brief the sheriff," she told him.

"Hold up." Will grabbed the cell phone off his desk. "I'm coming with you."

Sheriff Dillon Teixeira, whose spacious office was located on the other side of the building, was in his second term as sheriff of Dabs County, after previously working there as a sheriff sergeant. He was fifty-five years old, on a second marriage, and actually reminded Annette somewhat of her adoptive father, Taylor Lynley, both in his muscular stature and crusty blue-gray eyes. His silver hair was medium length with a side part.

"I was expecting you two," he said, dressed in his sheriff's uniform and seated at a large oak desk. "Got the autopsy report and scanned through it. Terrible that this case of a missing person had to end this way."

"Yeah, and the fact that her uncle, Trooper Hamilton McCade, has worked with us makes it all the harder," Will said.

"I agree," Annette echoed his sentiments. "I only just met Hamilton, but I feel for him and his sister, Maureen."

Teixeira rubbed his nose. "Same here. Mc-

Cade's one of us and deserves justice for his sister. As do the families of the other two young women we've lost recently, purportedly to the same killer." He leaned forward in his brown high-back leather chair and asked, "Where do things stand in the investigation on the latest homicide?"

Annette stepped toward the desk and responded candidly, "We're trying to put the pieces together on how Juliet McCade's vehicle ended up in a ditch with her dead inside the trunk. At this point, the best guess is that she was forced off the road and then someone attacked and killed her, leaving her to be found where she was. We have a possible lead on the unsub with the strand of hair removed by the medical examiner from Juliet's mouth." Annette glanced at Will and back. "It's been sent to the ISP crime lab for analysis and DNA, along with some personal items belonging to the victim that were uncovered at the crime scene."

"We also have a tire impression that may have come from the vehicle driven by the killer," Will pitched in. "It too has been handed to the state police crime laboratory to try and identify the tire and, ultimately, the car it belonged to and the driver."

"Sounds like some positive developments," the sheriff said, rubbing his hard jawline. "With any luck, this will give you the solid evidence needed to pinpoint the young woman's killer. Which, in turn, can allow us to nail the Christmas Lights Killer that appears to be one and the same."

"That's the plan," Annette said, smoothing an eyebrow. She realized that it was anything but a done deal as each potential angle could lead to nowhere. The last thing she wanted was to go back to square one in chasing down a serial killer, as that would only be playing right into his hands. And at the expense of Juliet McCade and the two other victims they believed had been targeted by the unsub.

HAMILTON SPENT THE afternoon doing his regular shift in patrolling his district. Of all the things about his job, he probably best liked the solitude, which gave him time to think and then digest his thoughts. In this case, it was all about losing his one and only niece, depriving Juliet of the chance to be a big-sister-like cousin to his own children. Assuming he was fortunate to one day have some kids with the right partner. Annette entered his mind as someone he found himself attracted to, in spite of knowing little about her. She was definitely his type and could be a good fit if things fell into place. But, for now, he needed to stay strong for Maureen.

He had acquiesced to her wishes and returned to work against his better judgment. If nothing else, it gave him something to focus on other than Juliet's murder as he looked for any activity that drew his attention. All seemed quiet and normal.

When he finished his shift, Hamilton drove to the Indiana State Police District 22 Police Department on Ellison Road. There, he met with his commander, Lieutenant Tony Wilson. African American and in his late forties, Wilson had deep sable eyes and was tall, bald beneath his campaign hat, and built like a brick wall inside his uniform. Hamilton informed him about his niece's murder in Carol Creek.

"Sorry to hear that," Wilson remarked as they stood in the building. "If you need some time to deal with it—"

"I don't," Hamilton cut in. At least not where it pertained to sitting around moping. "But I would like to be available to help in the investigation any way I can, as long as the killer remains on the loose."

The lieutenant's brow furrowed. "I understand how you feel, McCade. But getting involved in cases where it's personal is usually not a good idea. Besides that, this investigation is under the jurisdiction of the Dabs County Sheriff's Department. Wouldn't want to step on any toes, unless invited to."

"Juliet was my sister's only child, so, yes, it's definitely personal," he readily admitted. "But I'm enough of a professional to be able to separate the two. As far as stepping on toes, that shouldn't be a problem, either," Hamilton told him straightforwardly. "I'm already acquainted with the lead investigator on the case, Detective Annette Lynley, and her coinvestigator, Detective Will Hossack. With three murders believed to be connected, I'm guessing that they would welcome any assistance that comes their way." Even if not on the sheriff's payroll, he still wanted to work the case to the extent possible in finding Juliet's killer.

Wilson studied him for a moment. "Let me give Sheriff Teixeira a call and see where they're at in the investigation," he said deliberately, "and get back to you on this."

"Okay." Hamilton didn't want to make any waves. It wouldn't serve any purpose in fighting his commander on this. Especially when wanting his support as Hamilton hoped to get into the ISP's Investigations Command Special Investigation Section. He would work around his official duties, if necessary, till Juliet's killer was behind bars.

Hamilton drove his duty vehicle home, still

contemplating the multiple things weighing on his mind. He lived in a three-bedroom contemporary house on Hatcher Pass. Attracted to the turn-key modern structure, finished daylight basement and spacious backyard with crabapple and yellowwood trees, he'd purchased it just over a year ago.

He used the remote to open the two-car garage and pulled up next to his personal car, a red GMC Acadia Denali.

Entering the house, where Hamilton had a Christmas wreath on the front door, he stepped onto ceramic tile flooring and took in the spacious and open setting with floor-to-ceiling windows and plantation shutters, wood-burning fireplace and country furniture. A nice-sized concolor white fir tree sat in the living room, decorated for Christmas. He had picked it out at the DeLuca Christmas Tree Farm and roped a fellow trooper, Al Hernandez, into helping him get the tree back to his house. The French country kitchen had quartz countertops and stainless steel appliances, and a den on the floor had been converted into an exercise room. He removed his hat and headed up the quarter-turn staircase. After washing up in the owner's suite, he went back downstairs and heated up yesterday's leftover chili, before downing it with a couple of slices of bread and a beer.

I'd love to have someone to share this space with, Hamilton told himself, sitting at the pine dinner table in an upholstered side chair. Or maybe share her space elsewhere. Eating alone had never been fun. But it had been this way more often than not since his breakup with Felicity. He had gotten used to it. Yet he was in no way content. If Juliet's death showed him anything, it was that tomorrow was not promised to anyone. No matter how much things appeared to be in your favor in life. He would do well to remember that as he went through the motions of his professional life while hoping to kick-start his personal one.

Chapter Five

Should she or shouldn't she? Annette posed this question to herself as she weighed whether or not to call Hamilton to let him know she was en route to the Indiana State Police Fort Wayne Regional Laboratory in his neck of the woods. Yes, she wanted to keep him in the loop. But it would be presumptuous of her to just expect him to drop everything to meet up with her. On the other hand, if it were her and she'd just lost her niece to what was most likely a serial killer, she would definitely want to be kept abreast of every development—in person, if possible. The fact that it meant they got to see each other again was immaterial, if not something she welcomed as a chance to run into the good-looking trooper who'd captured her fancy.

Opting to make the call, Annette put her cell phone on speaker as it sat in the car holder. "Hey, Hamilton," she said evenly, when he answered.

"Hey." He sounded wary. "What's up?"

"I wanted you to know that I'm on my way to the Indiana State Police crime lab to get the results on evidence involving Juliet's death. If you're not too busy, you might want to join me, and we can see if they have anything that might point toward the killer."

"Absolutely," he responded without prelude. "I can swing over to the lab and meet you there."

"Good," she said, hoping he got her drift. She only meant good as it related to his availability for a common cause.

"So, what will we be looking at?"

"DNA from a hair found in Juliet's mouth, for one," Annette said keenly, while hoping DNA other than the victim's might show up as well among her recovered personal effects. "And a tire track that might have come from the unsub's vehicle."

Hamilton waited a beat, then said tonelessly, "Okay. See you soon."

She disconnected the call and continued to drive, pondering what it would take to capture the Christmas Lights Killer and return life to normal in Carol Creek. A good step in the right direction would be the results from the crime lab, she thought, pulling into the parking lot off Ellison Road. She spotted Hamilton's car with him in it. He got out when she did and they met halfway. "Hi," she said meekly, feeling as if he were towering over her, which wasn't necessarily a bad thing.

"Hey." He eyed her beneath the brim of his hat. "Let's see what they have to say."

She nodded and they went inside the building. In the Forensic Biology Section, greeting them was forensic scientist Kelly Okamoto, in her white lab coat. In her early thirties, she was slender and had short, sandy-colored hair with a small ponytail and brown eyes. "Detective Lynley. Trooper McCade," Kelly acknowledged them.

"Hey, Kelly," Annette said, having met her previously during other investigations.

"Kelly," Hamilton spoke from acquaintance.

"Sorry to hear about your niece," she said.

He nodded. "Hopefully, you have something that can identify her killer."

"Yes and no," Kelly uttered vaguely, leading them to her workstation. "We were able to collect DNA from the strand of hair extracted from the victim."

"That's good to know," Annette told her, having anticipated as much.

"The forensic unknown profile was entered into the state database with arrestee and convicted offender profiles," Kelly said, "as

well as DNA profiles from crime scenes."
She frowned. "Unfortunately, we didn't find a
match. The DNA profile has been recorded in
the National DNA Index System in the hope
that there will be a hit in CODIS. We'll just
have to wait and see."

Annette hid her disappointment that the DNA
didn't identify a suspect in the death of Juliet
McCade. She could see that it didn't set well
with Hamilton, either. But now that the DNA
profile was in CODIS, it meant they had something to work with should matching results
show up later from the unsub. "Were you able to
get DNA from Juliet McCade's personal items,
such as her cell phone and driver's license?" she
asked the forensic analyst.

"Yes, but it was only a match for the victim's
DNA," Kelly answered. "We're still running
tests, in case something else shows up."

"If it happens, keep us informed," Hamilton
advised her.

"Of course."

Annette looked at her. "Is there anything else
you can tell us about the hair?"

Kelly jutted her chin. "Yeah, we could deter-
mine that the hair almost certainly belonged to
a white male."

*Which, in and of itself, narrows down the lists
of potential suspects*, Annette thought.

They left that section of the crime lab with more information than when they'd entered, though less than what they would have wanted ideally, and went inside the Microanalysis Unit, where they analyzed fibers and tire impressions, among other things.

HAMILTON WOULD HAVE loved it if there had been a hit on the hair strand pulled from Juliet's mouth. In his gut, he felt it belonged to the person who'd murdered his niece. But apparently, the unsub had managed to avoid any arrests or incarceration in Indiana up to this point. But he'd made a mistake in providing them with his DNA, which gave Hamilton hope that it was only a matter of time before they knew precisely who they were dealing with. He sensed that Annette felt the same.

In the Microanalysis Unit, they met with forensic analyst Bernard Levinson, twentysomething and of medium build, with short black hair worn in a faux hawk and blue eyes behind glasses. Annette wasted little time in asking him about the tire track. "What did it tell you about the tire?" she asked pointedly.

Levinson touched his glasses. "Well, we analyzed the cast made of the tire track," he replied matter-of-factly. "The impression tells me that it definitely comes from a good all-season, all-terrain tire."

That made sense to Hamilton, given that they were near wintertime. And had certainly been experiencing some winter weather of late. "Can you be more specific?"

"I believe it may be a Goodyear tire, but can't be any more specific at this point without further testing." He gazed at Annette. "I suggest, Detective Lynley, that you go to a tire center. They can probably match the tire tread cast positively to the manufacturer and the exact kind of tire this is."

"I'll do that," she agreed. "Is there a tire center you can recommend?"

"I know one that's nearby," Hamilton told her. "I've done business with them and know the manager."

Annette smiled. "Let's check it out."

"Good luck," Levinson said.

"Thanks, Bernard," she told him. "You've given us a lead on the tire tread evidence. We'll see where it takes us."

Moments later, they took Hamilton's vehicle and headed to the tire center. It gave him an opening to get to know her a little better. "So, how did you end up working for the sheriff's department?" he asked curiously.

"I applied and got the job," she quipped. "As

I assume you did in going to work for the Indiana State Police."

"Walked right into that one." He grinned, having no issue with her dry sense of humor. But he still wanted to know more. "Let me rephrase it. How did you end up as a sheriff's department detective?"

"Oh, that's what you wanted to know. Why didn't you just ask?" she teased him.

"I'm asking now," he said levelly.

"Okay. I come from a family steeped in law and law enforcement. My adoptive parents were a police chief and criminal court judge, and two of my three siblings are FBI agents and the other is a law enforcement ranger with the National Park Service." Annette glanced his way. "Oh, and did I forget to mention that I have a first cousin who is an investigator for a correctional institution?"

Hamilton chuckled. "I can see why law enforcement would be in your blood." He could only imagine the interesting conversations they had during family get-togethers.

"Right." She giggled. "Having a bachelor's in criminology was a bonus as I worked my way through various jobs in policing before landing my current position as a detective."

"I see." It was obvious to him that even with the family pedigree, she had succeeded in her endeavors largely through her own hard work. As had he. "Have you ever thought about trying to contact your birth parents, assuming you haven't already been in touch with?" he wondered out of curiosity.

"I haven't been, but have thought about it," she voiced musingly. "Or at least my birth mother, since from what I was told, my father was never in the picture. Maybe someday, if the need is strong enough to want to go there for answers and clarity. Or maybe she'll reach out to me. For now, I'm happy to have been with those I'll always consider my family."

"Understood." He respected her fortitude and willingness to embrace the hand she had been dealt through no fault of her own.

"Your turn," Annette said, cutting into his train of thought. "How did you end up as a state trooper?"

"No bloodline to point me in the right direction," he answered wryly. "For whatever reason, I've always had an interest in law and order and education in that field. Got my bachelor's, master's, and eventually PhD, all in criminal justice, while working as an officer for the police department before spending the last decade as a trooper." He wondered if that was too much information for her interest.

"Impressive, especially the PhD," Annette said sincerely.

"Not all it's cracked up to be," Hamilton said, downplaying the achievement. "Still trying to decide how to make the most of it." He believed that getting into ISP's Organized Crime and Corruption Unit would be a good step in the right direction.

"I've thought about going back to school for my master's, though maybe in psychology or sociology, but haven't found the time to do so."

"I'm sure if you're serious about that, it will eventually work itself out," he told her.

"We'll see," she said thoughtfully.

Hamilton almost wished they hadn't arrived at their destination on Coldwater Road, as Annette had piqued his interest and he wanted to know more. Maybe they could pick this up later.

As they headed toward the tire center, their shoulders brushed. Hamilton felt something akin to an electrical current zip through his body in that instant. Did she feel it, too? Or was it only him that was being stirred by her mere presence and thoughts of what they could do were they alone, hot and bothered?

They went inside the store and were approached by Pete Lipton, the manager. "Hey, Pete," Hamilton said, eyeing the fortysomething, stocky man with a brown Ivy League haircut and gray eyes, who had serviced both his duty and personal vehicles.

He gave a nod. "How can I help you, Trooper McCade?"

"This is Detective Lynley with the Dabs County Sheriff's Department." Hamilton faced her. "She's working a case in which we're trying to pinpoint the tire tread found near a homicide."

"Hi, Detective," Pete said. "Happy to help, if I can."

"Thanks." Annette smiled at him. She showed Pete the cast of the tire track. "Can you identify the type of tire this would have come from?"

The tire center manager studied the tread. After a moment or two, he said equably, "I'm pretty sure this is from a Goodyear Wrangler Fortitude HT."

"Really?" She glanced at Hamilton and back. "Take another look."

Pete did and reached the same conclusion. "Just to be on the safe side, let me show it to my top mechanic, Clayton Serricchio."

They watched as Pete disappeared into the shop. "What do you think?" Annette asked Hamilton.

"I trust Pete's knowledge when it comes to

cars and tires. No reason to believe he's off base. But a second opinion never hurts."

"True."

Pete returned in a moment and said, "Clayton took a look at the tire tread cast and backs me up. It *is* a Goodyear Wrangler Fortitude HT."

That was good enough for Hamilton. "Thanks for your help," he said.

"Anytime," Pete replied, shaking both their hands.

Outside, Annette said enthusiastically, "With the exact tire identification, we have an important lead to work with in trying to narrow down the vehicle it belonged to as well as the driver."

"I concur," Hamilton said, while tempering his anticipation that one thing would lead to another. "Hopefully, this will allow us to track down my niece's killer and not prove to be just an innocent driver who simply slipped on the road during wintry weather."

"My gut instinct tells me there's more to it than that," she insisted. "The timeline seems to fit the belief that the driver of that vehicle was involved with Juliet being forced off the road… and killed."

Hamilton knew all about the importance of gut instinct, as he relied on his own more often than not. Moreover, he sensed that Annette was onto something here. The sooner the driver could be questioned, the sooner Juliet's killer might be arrested and put behind bars.

"I'll take you back to your car," he told her.

The drive was mostly silent as she stared out the window and he mulled over having a greater role in the investigation and what he could do to help Maureen cope with her daughter's unexpected death.

WHEN ANNETTE RETURNED to Carol Creek and the sheriff's office, she had a mixed bag to report on the visit to the ISP Fort Wayne Regional Laboratory. They seemed a little closer to getting some answers as to who may have killed Juliet McCade, but weren't quite there yet. On another front, she was still a bit shaken by the jolt she'd felt when brushing shoulders with Hamilton outside the tire center. By his reaction, she was sure he experienced the sensation, too. There was no denying that she felt a connection with Hamilton that Annette knew needed to be explored, one way or the other, assuming he was single and on the same wavelength. But first, she needed to stay on track to solving his niece's murder and presumably getting the jump on a serial killer at the same time.

She briefed Sheriff Teixeira in his office on the results from the crime lab. "The DNA may eventually yield some results on who the hair came from. But the Goodyear Wrangler Fortitude HT tire track found near the scene of the crime is solid," she told him. "It could be the break we need to get some real answers."

"I think you may be right about that," Teixeira said, leaning against a corner of his desk. "But with three women dead in the same manner in our town and attributable to a lone killer, we have to assume that the unsub is still on the hunt for others. Meaning there's no time to spare in tracking him down. I'll reach out to the ISP for further assistance in dealing with this serious matter. And even the FBI."

I was hoping you'd say that, Annette thought, wishing her brothers with the Bureau were operating out of the Indiana field office instead of their own respective locations. As it was, she knew that every second counted before the perp might strike again. She wondered if Trooper Hamilton McCade would be called upon to assist in the investigation into his niece's killer. Or would it hit too close to home for him to go deeper into the probe?

"In the meantime," Teixeira continued, "I'll pull Detective Robinson from the cold case she's working on and get Reserve Deputy Shelton Kuen to help out."

"I appreciate that," Annette said, happy to have all the aid they could get in bringing this investigation to a close with an arrest of the culprit. She was sure Will would agree and that Detective Charisma Robinson would not object to putting on hold a thirty-year-old homicide case involving a murdered husband and wife in favor of solving a current serial killer case. "The more feet on the ground, the better."

"Right." Teixeira nodded. "Let's make this count, Detective," he said in no uncertain terms.

"Yes, sir," Annette told him respectfully, while knowing that she was under the gun for delivering results as the lead detective and still trying to get her feet wet with the Detective Bureau. She certainly was not about to throw in the towel on this investigation anytime soon. Not when women were dying and the killer seemed to be daring them to catch him as if he were a chameleon. Annette felt certain it was only a matter of time before they got him. It was the interim period that worried her for the safety of women in Carol Creek.

In her office, Annette closed the door and sat at the desk. She took her cell phone and called her sister, Madison Lynley, for a video chat. Madison was nearly two years her senior and they were not quite as close as Annette was to Russell, but they were the only girls among the siblings. It gave them a special bond, and she was someone Annette knew she could always count on and be herself with.

When Madison appeared on the small screen, her attractive face and bold aquamarine eyes lit up. "Hey, sis," she said cheerfully.

"Hey." Annette could see that she was standing in uniform near the Blue Ridge Parkway in North Carolina, where Madison was stationed as a law enforcement ranger. "Busy?"

"I can spare a few minutes to talk," she said, her long blond hair with bangs worn in a bun. "How are things?"

Annette twisted her lips. "Truthfully, they could be better."

"Russell mentioned to me that you were dealing with a missing woman and a serial killer on the loose," Madison noted. "Is there more, not to say that this isn't enough on your plate?"

"Well, the cases have merged into one," Annette told her sadly. "The missing woman, Juliet McCade, turned up dead and we believe she was a victim of the serial killer."

Madison frowned. "Sorry to hear that. Makes my own workload primarily involving rowdies, substance abusers, car accidents and wounded animals seem not so bad. So, how is the investigation shaping up?"

Annette filled her in on a few details, including the tire track evidence, and then mentioned casually, "Juliet's uncle, a state trooper named Hamilton McCade, has been involved in the investigation somewhat."

"Trooper McCade, huh?" Madison picked up on her hint that there was possibly more to this. "Is he good-looking?"

"Hadn't really noticed," she lied, chuckling at the absurdity of it. "Okay, yes, he's hot. Burning up, in fact," Annette admitted. "But I know nothing about his marital status or availability, so I'm not even going there." Not yet anyway.

"Hmm..." Madison seemed less than convinced. "If you say so. Far be it for me to give any advice in matters of the heart."

Annette knew that, like her, Madison had endured a painful breakup not so long ago, and was still coming to terms with it. But they were both strong Lynley women and would eventually find the right guy to make a life with. "I'll keep you posted on whether anything emerges with the trooper. For now, we're just professional acquaintances."

"Fair enough," her sister said, not pressing the issue.

They spoke briefly about the still-ongoing plans to meet up for Christmas, and then Annette ended the video chat. She mused about Hamilton for a moment and the sense of urgency in finding his niece's killer, before she called Will and brought him up to date on her visit to the crime lab and tire center.

Chapter Six

"How are you doing?" Hamilton hesitated to ask his sister over the speakerphone while on patrol, as the reality settled in about Juliet. But he needed to know that she was okay, even as the investigation into his niece's death continued.

"I'm fine," Maureen responded. He doubted that but took it as a sign that she was trying to cope as best as possible. "I just wish Juliet had been given a chance to reach her full potential in life."

"I know." He winced at the thought that this wouldn't be the case. "She made the most of the time she had," he said, truly believing this, as Juliet had always been more mature than her years and shown a willingness to go the extra mile in trying to achieve her goals.

"I suppose. But that doesn't make losing her to the whims of a killer any easier."

I can't dispute that, Hamilton thought, driving down the highway. "You're right." He paused, debating whether or not to mention the leads the sheriff's office had in tracking down the unsub. The last thing he wanted was to get her hopes up that an arrest was imminent. "I won't rest till her killer is brought to justice," he promised.

"That's good to know," Maureen said. "If it is the same serial killer on the loose in Carol Creek, he needs to be stopped so other mothers and fathers won't have to go through what I'm experiencing."

If only I could guarantee that no one else would die before the perp was caught, Hamilton mused. But considering he wasn't even part of the official investigation as yet, his options for working the case were limited. That didn't mean he wouldn't give it his all to do whatever he could to get the desirable results in allowing Juliet to rest in peace. "Why don't you come spend a few days at my house," he told his sister, believing it might do her some good to step away from the place where she'd been living with Juliet and the memories associated with it. "This is a time when we should be able to lean on one another in closer proximity."

"I appreciate the offer, Hamilton," she said, "but I need to be here. I have my job, for one, just as you do, and it gives me something else to focus on. Having a longer commute to work wouldn't help. Apart from that, my entire support group, other than you, is in Carol Creek."

It was a bad idea, Hamilton conceded, realizing that trying to shield her from further pain by pulling her away from her comfort zone and work as a registered nurse at Carol Creek General could do more harm than good. "I understand," he said. "Shouldn't have suggested it."

"You had every right to," she insisted. "I know you're just trying to help and you are. Juliet always looked up to you as her uncle. We're both hurting and trying to adapt to this new reality."

"Yeah," he said broodingly. He had forgotten how insightful his sister was. She was also hardened somewhat from everything she'd gone through over her lifetime. Maureen would need that fortitude as she tried to forge ahead for a life without her daughter. Hamilton steeled himself to have the same courage, though his heart ached at the thought of his niece whom he used to tease and offer advice whenever she needed it.

At the end of his shift, he went into the ISP District 22 building, where Hamilton was summoned to his commander's office. Lieutenant Tony Wilson was leaning over a solid wood adjustable standing desk when he walked in. Hamilton glanced around the space with ergonomic office furniture and a picture window. He turned back to the lieutenant, who said, "Just got off the phone with Sheriff Teixeira. His office has requested our assistance in their investigation of the Christmas Lights Killer. I take it you believe he's the one responsible for your niece's murder?"

"The MO suggests as much," Hamilton replied candidly.

"I see." Wilson stepped toward him. "You did your dissertation on serial killers, right?"

"Yeah." He was impressed that the lieutenant remembered after a brief conversation about it.

"Then that should make you an asset to the sheriff's detectives who are investigating the homicides. Go ahead and lend them your expertise and, hopefully, help apprehend a serial killer. Of course, you'll be continuing your official duties for the ISP."

"Will do, on both counts." Hamilton gave a nod and felt an adrenaline rush at the prospect of doing more to help Annette chase down Juliet's killer. Not to mention another opportunity to spend more time with the striking, thought-provoking detective.

ANNETTE GOT A text from Hamilton, informing her that he'd been recruited to work with them on the Christmas Lights Killer case. She was pleased to hear this, assuming that his primary role would be employing investigative skills as a longtime state trooper to help in the interviewing of suspects and surveying the crime scenes for any clues left behind. If their prior interactions were any indication, she was sure they would get along fine. And actually complement one another for a common cause in going after his niece's killer.

Annette glanced at Hamilton as he entered the Detective Bureau's conference room that afternoon, where the team was gathered. He gave her a nod and seemed all business in his trooper hat and uniform. As lead investigator, she stood before them to provide a briefing on the case. Taking a quiet breath while calming her nerves within, she said, "We're here to bring everyone up to date on where things stand in the Christmas Lights Killer investigation. As of today, three young women have been the victims of ligature strangulation deaths by what we believe to be an adult male serial killer."

She turned on the slide presentation and used a stylus pen to show a facial image of an attractive white female with big blue eyes and long blond hair. "JoBeth Sorenson was a twenty-seven-year-old English teacher at Carol Creek High School," Annette said. "On December first, Sorenson's Honda Insight broke down on

Shadow Lane. Someone picked her up, drove her to an out-of-the way area on Brockton Drive, then strangled her with Christmas string lights, which seem to be garden-variety and easily accessible. Hard to pinpoint where they originated from. A witness reported seeing the victim in a dark vehicle with a man shortly before the estimated time of death."

Annette switched to a picture of a man in his late twenties with blue eyes, dark textured wavy hair and a patchy beard. "Sorenson's ex-boyfriend, Aaron Heathcote, was initially considered a person of interest in her murder, but he had an unshakable alibi, putting us back to square one." She turned to an image of a Hispanic female with big hazel eyes and thick blond hair worn in a pixie bob. "Yancy Machado is a twenty-five-year-old makeup artist. On December fourth, she was strangled to death with string Christmas lights by someone who accosted her in the parking lot of Machado's apartment complex on Winchester Street. A witness reported seeing a man run from the scene, but she didn't get a good look at him, aside from describing him as a tall white male with dark hair."

Annette sighed as she prepared herself to talk about the last known victim, hoping it wouldn't be too hard for Hamilton to listen to the nightmarish details all over again. Putting his niece's picture on the screen, and recognizing again the similarities between herself and Juliet as biracial, gave Annette a chill. Under other circumstances, it just as easily could have been her who fell into the crosshairs of a serial killer. "On December eighth, Juliet McCade, a twenty-one-year-old sales clerk at a boutique, went missing shortly after she texted her mother, Maureen McCade, to say she thought someone was following her. A search ensued for Juliet, to no avail. Two days later, her body was found in the trunk of her Subaru Impreza, which was stuck in a ditch off Murdon Street." Annette paused, averting Hamilton's hard stare. "She had been the victim of ligature strangulation, with Christmas string lights the murder weapon, same as the previous two victims of the so-called Christmas Lights Killer."

Using the stylus, Annette pointed to an image of a strand of hair on the screen. "This hair was pulled out of Juliet McCade's mouth. We believe it belongs to her killer. We were able to extract DNA from the hair. Unfortunately, it doesn't match any profiles in the state or national databases. It's an important lead, nonetheless." She replaced the image with an image of the tire tread cast. "Someone left this track not far from where Juliet's vehicle was found. The Indiana State Police crime lab and a tire center were able to identify the imprint as belonging to a Goodyear Wrangler Fortitude HT. We believe that whoever was driving the vehicle with this tire may well be the unsub. Or, at the very least, a possible witness. Needless to say, we're trying to locate the car and driver."

Annette waited a beat before saying, "It seems probable that the victims have been chosen randomly. As such, the age range and differences in their racial or ethnic persuasion are likely immaterial to the perpetrator, but rather more a reflection of being opportunistic when a target was available to go after at the right time and place."

She faced Hamilton and held his gaze, realizing that he was eyeing her with understanding and resolve rather than vexation or disappointment, where it concerned talking candidly about his niece. When it came time for them to switch places, he indicated as much, whispering in Annette's ear, "Thanks for more than adequately summing up the case for relative newbies like me. Juliet's death and its horrific nature can't be lessened, if we're to get to the bottom of this."

"You're right," she agreed, but was happy to hear him say it nonetheless. "We all have a job to do, even when it hurts sometimes. Thank you for the support."

He flashed her a genuine look. "Anytime."

Annette took that for what it was worth and gave him the floor as she took a seat at the conference table, curious as to what he hoped to bring to the investigation besides devilish good looks and a strong desire to go after the unsub.

HAMILTON WAS HAPPY to be able to contribute in any manner to solving the mystery of his niece's death. He owed this to Juliet and Maureen to do right by them in assisting the sheriff's department with their investigation. Working the case with Annette Lynley was obviously an added benefit to him, as they seemed to click on some level, though he was still sorting out in his mind to what degree. It wasn't lost on him that being biracial, she resembled Juliet in her physical characteristics. He wondered if this was why she appeared to take Juliet's death almost as personally as he did, believing it could have been her own daughter, assuming she had one. Or even herself at a younger age. Either way he sliced it, Annette had gotten his attention and Hamilton felt they had a common cause that he wanted to see through, wherever it might lead.

He surveyed the others in attendance beyond fellow ISP investigators brought on for the serial killer case. Some he knew, and others he hoped to get to know professionally. "I'm Hamilton

McCade," he introduced himself. "Juliet McCade's my niece." He let that set in for a moment. "Obviously, it's been a trying time for me and my sister, Juliet's mom, coming to grips with what happened to her. But we're dealing with the tragedy as best as possible, much like the families of the other victims of this killer who are going through the same thing."

Hamilton certainly didn't want this to be a pity party. He was there to work and not linger over his own misfortune. "I've had the privilege of working with a few of you over the years as a state trooper," he said. "What you probably didn't know was that I have a PhD in criminal justice from Indiana University Bloomington and did my dissertation on serial killers and what drives them. I suppose that makes me a serial killer profiler, which is where I hope to provide some insight into what you're up against in going after this monster."

Hamilton eyed Annette, who looked surprised in learning this new dimension of him as a trooper and person. He didn't necessarily hope to impress her, but imagined it didn't hurt matters any to know that he brought more to the table than his investigative skills, though ever present in his line of work. "Let me just start by saying that as it relates to a general profile of the unsub we're dealing with, the vast majority of serial killers tend to be male. Other than that, they run the gamut in terms of age range, mental stability, intellect, educational level, occupation, motivation, etc. In this particular investigation, there is nothing unique about the serial killer known as the Christmas Lights Killer, putting aside his deliberate use of indoor string Christmas lights to strangle his victims. I believe this is more for shock effect, if anything, given that the murders are occurring during the Christmas season in Carol Creek. But the truth is, history is replete with serial killers who, by definition, have killed two or more persons on separate occasions. Even the ligature strangulation killings are quite common, historically speaking. The so-called Boston Strangler, who may have been more than one person, Hillside Stranglers, Green River Killer, Tourniquet Killer, to name a few, murdered many, if not all, their victims by ligature strangulation.

"So, what's the motivation for this madness?" Hamilton posed the question he suspected they were probably wondering. "Well, once you put aside the often random nature of such attacks and the opportunity to commit them, as Detective Lynley alluded to on the current case, for most serial killers it really comes down to a general dislike for the victims or someone they represent, usually as a reflection of feeling wronged by the person or persons. This loathing, and anger by virtue, can manifest itself through psychotic or sadistic behavior, leading to retaliatory or get-even attacks against those who epitomize the object of hatred. When there's a sexual component to the killings, the perpetrators will often resort to sexual assaults or other forms of sexual appeasement as indicative of their holding power over the victims and imposing their will on them."

Hoping his understanding of serial killers would help his audience with nabbing the Christmas Lights Killer, Hamilton continued. "In targeting young women, the unsub we're dealing with here seems to generally conform to everything I've outlined in terms of motivation, MO, opportunity and an escape route. He has also been smart enough to keep the evidence that could identify him to a minimum. Obviously, that's starting to wane, since he's gotten sloppy by purportedly leaving DNA and tire tread evidence that may well prove to be his undoing. Short of that, the unsub is all but certain to go after other victims who fit his criteria for killing."

After answering a few general questions, Hamilton let Will Hossack take over. As they passed one another, Will quipped, "You really know your stuff, McCade. Why have you been hiding that?"

Hamilton smiled ruefully. "It's always been there. Just never been called upon to apply it to a real-life case."

"You couldn't have picked a better time to lay it out there," the detective said. "For your niece and the other victims of the Christmas Lights Killer, we definitely need all hands on deck if we're to crack this before Christmas."

"That would be great," Hamilton said, walking away. Knowing that Juliet would not get to spend Christmas with Maureen or him was motivation enough. Hoping to avert the same sad outcome for other families gave him even more reason to see the killer stopped cold.

"You're full of surprises," Annette caught his attention after the meeting had ended.

He kept an even keel while responding, "Seemed like as good a time as any to say what I needed to."

"I agree. Maybe you could enlighten me even further."

He cocked a brow. "Maybe. What did you have in mind?"

She smiled teasingly. "Can I buy you dinner, if you don't have other plans? And please don't say you'd rather buy me dinner instead. That's so old-school."

Hamilton chuckled. She was right. Women were just as capable of wining and dining men as vice versa. He had absolutely no problem with that. In this case, having dinner with her under any circumstances was something he looked forward to. He told her lightheartedly, "Far be it for me to go old-school on you. I accept. Dinner it is, your treat."

She laughed. "Was hoping you'd say that."

"Your wish is my command," he said, feeling that the cliché was apropos for the moment, while meaning every word.

Chapter Seven

Annette had admittedly acted on impulse when inviting Hamilton to dinner. It had seemed like a good idea at the time, after he had blown her away with his insight on serial killers and what drove them. Applying his knowledge to the Christmas Lights Killer case could help law enforcement do their job that much faster. Apart from that, she wanted to get to know the trooper better and see if there really was anything there that warranted pursuing him. Or, for that matter, being pursued by him. She was happy that he didn't make a fuss over the who-should-pay-for-dinner thing as some guys might have. As it was, she was more than capable of buying someone she invited a meal. If things were to move in the right direction for them, she was even open to cooking him a meal one day.

They drove their separate vehicles to the Steak Train, a popular restaurant not far from the sheriff's office. Once seated at a table by the window, Hamilton removed his hat, fully revealing for the first time his coal-colored hair in a military high and tight hairstyle. Annette imagined running her fingers through and across it, as he picked up his menu and ordered the ribeye with mushroom gravy along with a garden salad and cheese fries, and lemonade to drink.

"Might as well go the distance since you're buying," he said, a crooked grin on his face.

Annette laughed. "Feel free to do so," she responded, owning up to her offer to foot the bill. She ordered the roasted lamb shank, a Caesar salad and coffee. As they waited for the food and drinks, she dove right into the thing foremost on her mind. "So, is there a Mrs. Hamilton McCade? A girlfriend? Any children?"

"That's a mouthful. Fortunately, we're not eating yet." Hamilton chuckled at his own humor. "No Mrs. No girlfriend. No children. Juliet was the closest thing I've had to a daughter, up to this point." He paused just long enough for Annette to feel relieved, if not elated, that he was single. As if to zero in on this, he said reflectively, "I was in a relationship with a woman named Felicity Sheridan six months ago, but it ended when she decided to hedge her bet with an investment banker she met online."

Annette frowned. "Sorry about that," she

said, but felt that his ex had given up more than she had gained in dumping the handsome trooper.

Hamilton shrugged. "Don't be. It happens. Better she showed her true colors earlier than later."

"I agree." She was glad he was able to put it behind him and move on. Not everyone could.

They were interrupted when the drinks arrived, after which Hamilton took up the conversation once again. "Now why don't you tell me your relationship status... Any kids, etc.?"

Annette sighed. "Single and never married," she told him, sipping her coffee. "My last boyfriend, Eric Rodriguez, cheated on me with someone he worked with." The memory still stung, even though she'd gotten him out of her system. "I don't have any children," she added. *Though I would certainly be open to becoming a mother with the right father,* she thought inwardly.

Hamilton sat back with his drink musingly. "Your ex was an idiot."

"I know, right?" She smiled. "There are more than a few idiots out there," she added, alluding to his ex as well.

"Yeah." He chuckled. "Where did you grow up? I'm sensing it wasn't Indiana?"

"Your senses are correct. I grew up and was

raised in Oklahoma," Annette said proudly. "My family still has property there."

"I've never been to Oklahoma, but as a big college football fan, I do follow the Oklahoma Sooners."

She flashed her teeth. "Good to know."

"Do you get back there much?"

"Not much," she admitted. "My parents have passed away and my siblings are all living elsewhere."

"I see." He tasted the lemonade. "My parents are gone, too. They weren't around very much even when alive," he muttered. "It was pretty much just me and Maureen, till Juliet came along."

"What about her father?" Annette asked curiously, hoping her question wasn't too intrusive.

"He was never in the picture." Hamilton wrinkled his nose in regret. "Maureen chose to go it alone in raising Juliet. I pitched in to help as much as I could."

Annette suspected that he had been a good uncle, as well as being a good brother. Now he and Maureen must've lost a good part of the bond they had and would need to rely more on one another to fill the void. Just as Annette felt was the case between her and her siblings after the death of their parents. But ultimately, each of them had to rely on their own inner strength to get over the hump. As Hamilton would need to do in the face of his tragedy.

After the food came and they dug in, Annette turned the subject matter back to Hamilton's dissertation. "What made you decide to take up serial killers to study?"

He lowered his chin. "I guess you could say I've always been a little morbidly curious about the subject—why some people kill as many as they can get away with, before being apprehended, killed or committing suicide rather than be made to answer for their crimes. As such, it seemed like worthwhile subject matter to tackle in my dissertation."

"You certainly have a good foundation on this type of criminal," she said, and sliced the knife into her roasted lamb shank.

"At least enough to have some clue as to what pushes their buttons, so to speak," Hamilton said, forking a generous piece of the ribeye steak.

Annette leaned forward. "Do you think this guy we're looking at could be someone acquainted with the victims as opposed to a stranger or random killer?"

"It's always possible," he conceded. "Or at least could know someone who knew the victims and went from there as an opening." Hamilton dabbed a napkin to his mouth. "But if I were a betting man, which I try not to be, based on everything you've told me about this serial killer and his MO, the odds are that he's chosen to go after women outside his own social group but are still susceptible in some way to letting him in." Hamilton winced before uttering forlornly, "Juliet was a bright young woman. Her text to Maureen gave no indication that she knew who was following her. By the time she came to terms with just how dire the situation was, it was too late."

"But maybe not too late to get the unsub responsible for her death." Annette sat back. "We have clues that can lead to his arrest."

Hamilton nodded. "Yeah, that is something to shoot for."

Hopefully with achievable results, Annette told herself. "Did you ever consider joining the FBI?" she asked, lifting up lettuce with her fork. "I'm sure the Bureau would love to have you working for them as a criminal profiler." She imagined him working alongside her brothers in solving crimes on the federal level.

"I thought about it," he replied, sipping lemonade. "But it wasn't for me. I love my current job as a state trooper, being out in the field and making things happen. That being said, wanting to expand my horizons at this stage of my life, I recently applied to get into the Organized Crime and Corruption Unit within the ISP's Investigations Command Special Investigation Section. Still waiting for word on that."

"Good luck," Annette said, believing he would be great in any capacity of law enforcement he chose. But for now, she was glad to have met him as a handsome state trooper, uniform and all.

"Thanks." Hamilton regarded her curiously. "Think you'll ever make the jump to federal law enforcement, given your siblings' jobs with the FBI and National Park Service? Or maybe go after that graduate degree and take a different direction?"

I should've known that was coming, Annette thought. She tasted her coffee musingly and replied vaguely, "Anything's possible. My brothers and sister are always trying to get me to join them. Right now, I'm happy in my own lane with the sheriff's department. Whatever the future holds, I'll go with the flow. That includes furthering my education and seeing if it means changing courses careerwise."

"Sounds like a plan." Hamilton showed his teeth. She was immediately warmed by that, as Annette could tell that he was genuine. That was the type of person she wanted in her life. But was he interested in anything beyond working together to apprehend his niece's killer?

WHEN HAMILTON WALKED Annette back to her car, the only thing he could think of was wanting to kiss her. He had no doubt that her lips were most kissable. But was she willing to go down that road? And even beyond? Only one way to find out. Before he chickened out and lived to regret it, Hamilton gazed down at Annette and asked doubtfully, "Would it be inappropriate if I kissed you goodbye?"

Her lashes fluttered. "No more than if I kissed you goodbye," she teased him. "So, let's go for it."

"Yeah, let's," he concurred wholeheartedly.

Hamilton tilted his face at the perfect angle and brought his mouth down to hers. Their lips fit together like a romantic puzzle and they kissed. It rattled his bones as she opened her lips ever so much, daring him to do the same. He took the challenge and pulled her closer to him in the process, shielding the evening's chill with the heat emanating from their bodies.

Hamilton could feel his heart racing when he broke the lip lock, not wanting to risk ruining a good thing. And from what he could see, everything was good where it concerned Annette Lynley. "That was nice," he stated honestly.

"Yes, very nice," she said, putting a finger to her lips.

"Thanks for the dinner. Next time, it's on me, if that's okay with you," he added, unless she preferred to foot the bill on every occasion, if there was more wining and dining to come.

Annette giggled. "Yes, that's fine with me. Next time, you buy."

"Deal." Hamilton was just happy to know there would be a next time. And not necessarily as dinner between colleagues.

"See you when I see you," she said, smiled at him and then got into her car.

"Okay." He waited till she had driven off, before heading to his own vehicle, wondering if this could be the start of something special. No matter that they were brought together by the ugliness of his niece being murdered.

WHILE AT HER DESK, Annette was still thinking about kissing Hamilton yesterday after their get-to-know-each-other-better dinner. The kiss had left her tingling from head to toe, and her vivid imagination had kept conjuring up pictures last night and into the morning of what it would be like to make love to him. She dragged herself from the tantalizing thoughts when Will Hossack walked into her office.

"According to cell phone records," Will said, "on the day she died, Juliet McCade made several phone calls to a Chad Lawrence."

Annette checked her notes to correspond with memory and saw that they were a match.

"Hmm…" she muttered. "Maureen McCade said that Juliet's ex-boyfriend was Chad Lawrence."

"Wonder what they were talking about and why they were even talking at all that day?"

"I wonder the same thing," Annette said. "Especially since they supposedly broke up after Juliet found out he was cheating on her."

Will furrowed his brow. "Maybe we need to have a little chat with Lawrence and see what he was up to the night she died. And for that matter, if he happened to know any of the other victims of the Christmas Lights Killer."

"I'm with you," Annette agreed. They needed to cover all bases in trying to track down Juliet's killer. Though there was no evidence to indicate that Juliet was intimately acquainted with her killer and this perspective certainly went against the grain in the belief that the three murders attributed to a serial killer were likely random attacks, it didn't necessarily mean *all* the murders were random.

Annette knew that, generally speaking, most murder victims did know their attackers. According to the Justice Department, only around one in ten victims of homicide was murdered by a stranger. And for female murder victims, in particular, more than ninety percent of those killed by men were victims of someone known to them, with the Centers for Disease Control and Prevention reporting that over half of female murder victims in the country were killed by current or former intimate partners. As such, Annette took seriously any possibility that Juliet could have been murdered by someone she was romantically involved with.

Riding with Will, Annette was still pondering this when he said, "So, what do you make of Hamilton's take on who we might be dealing with here?"

"I think his insight is sound and has to be taken seriously in forming a profile of the Christmas Lights Killer," she replied matter-of-factly. "Given the nature of the attacks, whether random or not, this serial killer does seem to be operating with a definite chip on his shoulder."

"I was thinking the same," Will said, driving through an intersection before the light could change. "The victims may or may not be lulled by a false sense of security, but once the unsub can get the jump on them, his true nature comes out."

"Which is what scares me." Annette pursed her lips. "He's like a ticking time bomb. Every potential victim could trigger his rage at any time." *That's why we have to find him and try to prevent another woman from falling prey to his homicidal rage*, she told herself.

"Yeah, you're right about that." They arrived at the Carol Creek Shopping Center on Mulbrook Avenue and Will parked in the lot. "Let's go see what Lawrence has to say."

They headed inside the mall to the shoe store where Chad Lawrence was the assistant manager. Holiday shoppers were out in full force, reminding Annette that she had yet to buy Christmas gifts that she planned to bring to the family get-together. While she didn't want to go overboard, she would get something that her siblings would appreciate. Annette mused about the bleak Christmas in store for Maureen McCade and how much it would impact Hamilton with his own life.

In the Best Shoes Shop, Annette and Will approached a tall and husky man in his early twenties, with thick dark hair in a taper fade cut and brown eyes. The name tag on his red store shirt identified him as Assistant Manager Chad Lawrence.

"Can I help you?" he asked evenly.

Annette flashed her badge. "I'm Detective Lynley and this is Detective Hossack of the Dabs County Sheriff's Department. Mr. Lawrence, we'd like to ask you some questions about Juliet McCade."

Chad's eyes darted from one detective to the other. "I still can't believe she's dead," he claimed, standing flat-footed in gray-and-white sneakers. "But I'm not sure what you want from me..."

Will stepped up to him and said point-blank, "Juliet called you a number of times on the day she died. The last of those calls was approximately an hour before we believe she was murdered. You want to tell us what the calls were about?"

Chad stiffened. "We were thinking about getting back together," he asserted. "The calls were part of that."

Annette raised a brow with skepticism. "According to Juliet's mother, she dumped you for cheating on her." He didn't deny it. "Now you expect us to believe she was willing to take you back?"

"It's the truth," Chad maintained. "Yeah, I screwed up, okay. But I never stopped caring for her and wanted a second chance. Juliet seemed open to that." His chin drooped. "Someone stopped it from ever happening."

"Where were you on the night of December eighth, between seven thirty and nine thirty?" Will asked him.

"Right here," he responded immediately. "It's our busiest time of year. Worked all day. The manager, Nancy Ramos, can verify that."

Annette saw no wavering on his part to believe he was lying. "We'll need to speak to her," she told him nonetheless, to confirm his alibi.

Chad nodded. "No problem."

After he called the manager on his cell phone to come out from the back room, Annette asked him if he knew JoBeth Sorenson or Yancy Machado. Chad denied having ever met either woman. Once his alibi checked out, he was no longer considered a suspect in Juliet's death. To Annette, the ex-boyfriend of Hamilton's niece was just another victim of her tragedy, which had ended any second chance between them.

Chapter Eight

Hamilton had never felt comfortable attending a funeral, having been to one too many over the years. Not that anyone would welcome the opportunity to go to one, or think of it as something akin to an afternoon picnic. But this one was especially hard to digest, as it was his own niece's service before she was buried in the Carol Creek Cemetery. Maureen had wanted her to be laid to rest next to Hamilton's parents, hoping they would reconnect in the next world. *I'd like that, too*, he told himself, believing it was a time when their differences in life could be put behind for the greater good in eternal rest.

He noted that Annette and Will were in attendance. Hamilton suspected that at least in part their presence was to surveil mourners in the hopes that someone might stand out as the killer. As morbid as it was, it wasn't uncommon for unsubs to show up at funerals to achieve a perverse thrill from the kill while hidden in plain view. Had Juliet's killer decided to show up, rejoicing in his triumph?

The thought was sickening. Hamilton put an arm around Maureen in support as they sat in the front pew of the church. Juliet's casket was closed and ready for burial. The young pastor, Gretchen Chappell, delivered the eulogy and Hamilton was moved at seeing his niece, who had had her entire future stolen from her, being given Juliet's just due.

When the service ended, Hamilton walked over to Annette and Will, telling them solemnly, "Thanks for coming."

"We wanted to be here for you," Annette said softly.

"Yeah," Will agreed, adding, "and also keep our eyes open for anything or anyone that seemed off."

"I understand." Hamilton welcomed any part of the investigation into Juliet's killer. Even if it meant showing up at the funeral to scope out a potential unsub. Still, he believed the detectives' support was genuine. "After the burial, Maureen's having a few people over at the house. You're both welcome to come, if you like."

"We'll drop by for a bit," Annette told him, and squeezed his hand. Just touching her reminded Hamilton of their kiss two days ago. He wondered when they might give it another try.

"Okay." Hamilton spotted someone he needed to talk to. "Can you excuse me?"

"Of course," she said.

He raced toward the exit just in time to catch Rita Getzler, Juliet's best friend. "Rita," he called, and got her attention.

In her early twenties and African American, she was small with brown eyes and had brown-blond hair in double Dutch box braids. She faced him. "Mr. McCade."

"Hey." He had met her before, when she was hanging out with Juliet during one of his visits to see his sister. "Got a sec?"

Rita nodded and frowned. "I'm so sorry this happened to Juliet."

"We all are," he told her earnestly.

"I never should have asked Juliet to meet me at the Pear Pub that night," she moaned. "It's my fault that she ended up in a ditch and—"

Hamilton couldn't let her finish, interrupting by saying, "It's no one's fault. Certainly not yours. What happened to Juliet could have happened to anyone, anywhere. The only one responsible for her death is the person who thought he had the right to take her life. The important thing now is to try and figure out what we can do to bring her killer to justice."

"You're right." Rita sniffled and wiped a tear from her cheek. "How can I help?"

Glad you asked, he thought, and responded, "Did Juliet happen to mention in recent times that someone, perhaps from work or elsewhere, may have been following, stalking or harassing her?"

Rita thought about it. "Not really. Ever since she and Chad broke up, guys have been trying to hit on her, but she seemed to take it in stride. I don't recall her feeling threatened by anyone in particular."

Hamilton pondered Annette mentioning to him that Juliet was apparently at least considering getting back together with Chad, whose alibi for the time of her death had held up. "Did you happen to mention to anyone else the night Juliet died that you were planning to meet at the Pear Pub?"

"Just our friend, Samantha Vaugier, who was also supposed to meet us there," Rita told him.

"And did she?" Hamilton asked curiously.

"Yes. She brought along another friend, Alycia Torres. We had a few drinks while waiting for Juliet to show up. I tried texting her several times, but got no response." Rita's brow creased. "If we'd known Juliet was in trouble…"

"I know," he said, not wanting her and their other friends to feel guilty for something none of them could have anticipated. He gave Rita his card that had his work and cell numbers.

"If anything else comes to mind that you think might be helpful in the investigation, don't hesitate to call me."

"Okay," she agreed, before he let her go.

Hamilton went to be by his sister's side as they prepared to take Juliet to her final resting place, even while knowing he wouldn't be able to rest himself till her killer was held accountable.

ANNETTE PUT IN an appearance at the post-funeral gathering, where she conferred briefly with Maureen, assuring her that they were working night and day to bring Juliet's killer to justice. "It's only a matter of time before an arrest is made," Annette promised her, feeling this in her heart and soul.

"Thank you for your dedication to this," Maureen said. "I know Hamilton feels the same way."

Annette felt a tingle at the mere mention of his name. She was happy to be on the same team with him, even if they belonged to two different law enforcement agencies. Solving Juliet's murder, along with murders of the other two victims, was front and center. "I'm only doing the job I was hired for by the sheriff's office," she said unassumingly. "Juliet deserves no less."

Maureen nodded, and holding back tears,

went to join a tall, gray-haired man who seemed to hold an affection for her. Watching them as they shared an embrace, Annette felt as though she were spying, and turned away and went in search of Hamilton, who had made himself scarce since she arrived. Was he purposely avoiding her?

She had her answer when she found him in conversation with Will in the family room, where they were standing beside a bookshelf filled with books, amid contemporary furniture. The two were friends beforehand, she had to remind herself. Will was surely updating him on the case and any progress, or lack thereof.

"Hey, you two," she uttered, getting their attention.

Hamilton immediately turned her way, offering a handsome smile. "Annette," he greeted her. "Will was just telling me that you were about to pay a visit to the DeLuca Christmas Tree Farm in relation to the investigation."

"Yes." She wondered how much Will had told him. "We've learned that last year, the owners, Patrick and Paul DeLuca, purchased a set of Goodyear tires like the one corresponding to the tire track found near the crime scene, for their Chevrolet Silverado. Given the close proximity between the farm and where Juliet's vehicle and body were found, we need to see if one or the other DeLuca could be a killer."

"Hmm..." Hamilton cocked a brow musingly. "A couple of weeks ago, I bought a tree from their farm." His nose wrinkled at the thought. "I'd like to accompany you to question the brothers."

"You're welcome to," Annette responded. "But shouldn't you be here with Maureen as guests arrive?"

"It's starting to wind down here," he said. "If there's an arrest to be made, I want to be there to watch the handcuffs being put on the perp."

"Understandable," she had to admit, given his vested interest as both a member of their task force and the uncle of one of the serial killer's victims. By the looks of it, Maureen seemed to be in good hands with the man she seemed to be close to.

"Why don't you two check out the Christmas tree farm," Will suggested, pulling a hardcover book off the shelf haphazardly and putting it back. "In case we're barking up the wrong tree, no pun intended, I'll use the time to search for more vehicles locally that have on them the brand of Goodyear tires we're looking for."

"That works for me," Hamilton said quickly.

"Me, too," Annette agreed, believing they could cover more ground this way, along with the efforts currently underway by others involved in the investigation.

"Then it's settled," Will declared.

It wouldn't truly be settled in Annette's mind till there was a firm resolution to the case. In the meantime, partnering with Hamilton did have its advantages, she believed, as the stirring kiss they shared flashed in her head.

HAMILTON HAD EXPECTED Maureen to push back against his premature exit, believing that it was important to show a united front in grieving the death of their only living relative. Not only did his sister not fight him on this, but encouraged him to do his part in going after Juliet's killer. It was almost as if Maureen couldn't get him out of her house fast enough. Or was this only his imagination?

Whatever the case, Hamilton was more than up for investigating the DeLuca brothers in connection with Juliet's death. At the same time, it was disturbing to think that the owners of a farm that he had been going to for the last several years for Christmas trees could be involved in serial murders.

"So, I assume the tree you bought is in place?" Annette broke his daydreaming. He was driving.

"Yep." Hamilton said succinctly, lifting up the brim of his hat slightly.

"Fully decorated?"

"That, too." He hadn't known at the time that the Christmas season would turn into a bleak one with Juliet's death, though he doubted she would want him to attach negative associations to a holiday that she had loved for as long as Hamilton could remember. "How about you?" he asked Annette, imagining that she had a sprawling tree decorated to the hilt at her place.

"I decided not to put up a tree this year," she muttered defensively. "Or other decorations."

"Can I ask why?" He had some idea of what she might say.

"Between work and plans to spend the holidays in Oklahoma with my siblings, I suppose I just got lazy, and have been using those as justification not to decorate this year."

"I see what you mean," he admitted. "It can get to be a bit much at times. On the other hand, Christmas only comes once a year and is meant to be enjoyed at home and away from home. Decorations and all." He paused. "I'd be lying if I said this Christmas won't be quite the same without Juliet around to give her two cents on how I fared with the tree, lights and the rest. But I'd like to think she would have approved. And even volunteered to spruce up my house more."

"Maybe I will get a small tree after all," Annette suggested. "Though not necessarily from the DeLuca Christmas Tree Farm."

He got her point, given the potential implications where it concerned the farm. "If you do decide to put up a tree, I'd love to help you decorate it." Not to mention have a look at the place she called home. Especially the primary bedroom.

"Oh, would you, now?" she said, a teasing quality to her tone of voice.

"Yeah, sure." He chuckled. "I promise to keep my hands where you can see them."

Annette laughed. "We'll see."

Hamilton took that as a sign that she was still open to spending more time together in an intimate way, which he, too, was all for. And beyond that, once the investigation into Juliet's death had run its course.

ANNETTE WONDERED ABOUT putting up a tree. She imagined it might be fun to do so with Hamilton and have some hot chocolate as part of the experience. Beyond that, she would wait and see how things flowed between them, though if their kiss was a good indication, she saw things sizzling even more should they decide to go all the way. She warmed at the notion, but willed herself to keep it in check for the moment.

They pulled up to the DeLuca Christmas Tree Farm on Pinely Lane. Both she and Hamilton were armed, should they encounter trouble from the brothers. Or whichever one might have something deadly to hide. But there was no need to request backup at this point of the investigation. Or unnecessarily alarm customers on the farm. Then there was the element of surprise if they were, in fact, moving in the right direction.

In the parking lot, they noted a white Chevrolet Silverado with plates that corresponded to the vehicle belonging to the DeLuca brothers. A cursory glance inside and out showed nothing out of the ordinary. Annette looked at the tires. No sign of damage. Only the usual wear and tear. "What do you think?" she asked Hamilton.

"Hard to tell," he admitted. "Could've been used in the commission of a crime. Or not."

She agreed. "Let's hear from the DeLucas."

"Hope they're both around."

They soon found themselves moving between groves of concolor white firs, black hill spruce trees, and Scotch pine trees in search of the suspects. Annette suggested, "Maybe we should separate and cover twice as much ground."

"Good idea," Hamilton agreed. "I'll head in that direction." He pointed down a row of concolor white firs. "If you need me for any reason, just holler."

"Will do," she said, adding, "same to you."

He nodded and they went in different directions. She soon came upon a tall, well-built man in his thirties who had just assisted an elderly couple before turning to Annette. "Need help with anything?" he asked in a friendly voice.

She took a moment to size him up further. He had a round face, blue eyes and black locks in a bro flow hairstyle, and wore a dark brown parka coat over his clothing and black cap-toe boots. Showing her identification, Annette said, "Detective Lynley with the sheriff's department. Are you Patrick or Paul DeLuca?"

"Paul." His eyes narrowed. "What's this all about?"

"I'm investigating the murder of Juliet McCade that occurred very close to your Christmas tree farm."

His features softened. "Oh, yeah, I heard about that." He eyed her warily again. "What does this have to do with me?"

Annette met his hard gaze. "A tire imprint was recovered near the crime scene. We have reason to believe that the killer may have been driving a vehicle with Goodyear Wrangler Fortitude HT tires, such as the Chevrolet Silverado you own."

Paul's head snapped back. "You think me or my brother had something to do with that?"

"You tell me," she shot back at him guardedly.

"We're not killers, Detective," he insisted. "You're way off base here."

We'll see about that, Annette thought. "Would you mind submitting to a DNA swab, just to eliminate you as a suspect?" she asked gently.

"Not at all." Paul jutted his chin. "I have nothing to hide. Neither does Patrick. We're just hardworking Christmas tree farmers."

There was something about the sincerity in his voice that made her inclined to believe he was telling the truth. But the proof was in the pudding. "In that case, Mr. DeLuca, you have nothing to worry about," Annette said, while wondering if Hamilton was drawing the same conclusion with his brother.

HAMILTON RECOGNIZED PATRICK DELUCA the moment he laid eyes on him in the row of concolor white fir trees. He had bought his own Christmas tree from the man, who was in his midthirties and brawny, with blue eyes, a salt-and-pepper Verdi beard, and a dark quiff haircut.

When Patrick saw him, he approached with a crooked grin and said, "Hey, Trooper McCade.

Don't tell me you're back for another concolor white fir?"

"Not quite," Hamilton said, walking toward him. "I'm investigating the murder of my niece, Juliet McCade."

Patrick lifted a thick brow. "That was your niece?"

"Yeah." Hamilton could tell that he knew which murder they were talking about, given the proximity to the farm.

"Never made the association." Patrick scratched his beard. "Sorry for your loss, man."

That remains to be seen, Hamilton mused. "The killer was likely driving a vehicle with Goodyear Wrangler Fortitude HTs," he pointed out. "Much like the Silverado out in the lot. Is it yours?" Hamilton played dumb to see how he responded.

"Yeah, it belongs to me and my brother, Paul," Patrick confirmed. "It's used for the business. Definitely not for driving around to kill women."

"Mind telling me where you were the evening of December eighth?"

"Here," Patrick answered without prelude. "So was Paul. All day till closing at eleven p.m. There were plenty of customers coming and going who saw us," he insisted.

In his experience, Hamilton knew that a

clever killer could fake an alibi, even with witnesses. "Would you be willing to submit to a DNA test, if only to remove you from consideration as a suspect?"

"Hell yes, I'll take the test," Patrick said flatly. "So will Paul, if that will clear us."

"It will," Hamilton assured him with confidence, believing that the DNA they'd collected belonged to the unsub in Juliet's death. Now Hamilton needed to find Annette, compare notes, and see once and for all if the DeLuca brothers were innocent. Or if one or the other was guilty as sin.

Chapter Nine

With the DNA tests of Paul and Patrick De-Luca sent to the crime lab for analysis, Hamilton thought it was a good time to broach another subject on his mind as he dropped Annette off at the sheriff's office. "About that dinner I owe you…"

"Yes?" She eyed him with anticipation from the passenger seat.

"I'd love to cook you a nice dinner instead of buying you one," he said.

"You can cook?"

He laughed. "Don't look so surprised. I'm a man of many talents."

"Hmm…" Annette chuckled this time with a decided undertone. "I'll bet." She waited a beat before asking, "Are you inviting me to your house in Fort Wayne?"

He had seriously considered this. But with the driving distance and hazardous conditions, along with the current criminal investigation, it made more sense to stay within the parameters of Carol Creek. "Actually, I have a lakefront cabin in town," he told her. "I like to hang out there in the summertime, but it's pretty cozy during the colder months, too. It has a full-size kitchen and plenty of wood for the fireplace to keep warm, over and beyond the heating system. So, what do you say?"

Annette smiled. "I'd be delighted to have dinner at your cabin," she said spiritedly. "I don't get out to the lake very often, especially during wintertime."

"Then it's a date." Hamilton was sure they could call it that. "I can pick you up here or at your house. Whatever you're comfortable with."

"My house is fine." She gave him the address and they agreed he would show up at six thirty so they could proceed from there.

After he drove off, Hamilton found himself curious about her residence. Was there room enough for two? Especially in the primary bedroom? If he played his cards right, maybe he would get to find out firsthand.

But right now, he needed to pick up some groceries, double-check the firewood, and see to it that the cabin was presentable. Even that, though, would have to wait. He wanted to check in on Maureen and make sure she was holding up all right after the ordeal today of putting her only child in a grave.

When he drove back to her house, Hamilton noted that a blue BMW X5 was parked next to Maureen's Honda Odyssey. *Looks like not everyone has cleared out after the post-funeral gathering*, he told himself. He saw that as a good thing, since keeping his sister occupied was a good way to get her out of the funk she'd been in and back to living her life again. *Something I'm trying to do myself*, Hamilton thought, exiting his duty vehicle while thinking about his date with Annette.

He rang the bell and Maureen opened the door. "Hey," he said. "Wanted to make sure you're okay."

"I'm good, considering," she responded nebulously.

"If you've got company, I don't want to intrude." Even in saying that, he had no reason to believe she was romantically involved with anyone right now.

"Actually, I was hoping you would stop by again as I wanted to talk to you." Maureen opened the door wider. "Please come in."

Hamilton stepped inside the door. He was glad to see that she had left up the Christmas tree and other holiday decorations, knowing that Juliet would not have wanted it to be any other way. Out of his peripheral vision, he spotted movement and turned to the L-shaped sectional, where he saw a man sitting.

Maureen's visitor was in his fifties, and slim with short, gray hair in a low skin fade with a side part, gray-blue eyes behind rectangle glasses, and a gray goatee circle beard. Hamilton recognized him from the funeral as one of his sister's colleagues from work, a radiologist. What was his name?

Hamilton stretched his mind, before Maureen said coolly, "You remember Eddie Huston?"

"Yes," he told her. "Hey, Eddie."

"Hamilton." Eddie stood at nearly Hamilton's height and the two shook hands.

Maureen took a breath and asked her brother, "Do you want something to drink?"

Why do I feel you're holding back on me? Hamilton thought, meeting her eyes. "I'm good."

She fiddled with her hands and said gingerly, "Eddie and I have been seeing each other for a while now."

"Really?" Hamilton eyed the other man. "How long is a while?"

"A couple of months," she said.

"Why didn't you mention it before now?" he asked curiously.

"I wanted to see if it was going anywhere

first." Maureen made a face. "Apart from that, I didn't want to scare him off by you giving him the third degree, Mr. Trooper."

"Me?" Hamilton laughed uncomfortably. "I would only be looking out for you, not trying to run your life."

"I told her the same thing," Eddie pitched in with a chuckle. "But I guess your sister just didn't want things to be too weird between us."

"They won't be," he tried to assure her, while getting used to the idea that she was seeing someone. "Did Juliet know?" *Or had she also been kept in the dark?* he wondered.

"She knew," Maureen said evenly. "Juliet got along great with Eddie."

Is that so? How great? Hamilton asked himself, studying the radiologist. "Glad to hear," he muttered.

Eddie met his gaze. "Look, I want you to know that I truly care about your sister and I thought that Juliet was a good kid. I would never have wanted anything bad to happen to her." He paused. "And I certainly wouldn't have wanted to hurt Juliet myself in any way."

"I never said—" Hamilton started, even if he'd been thinking about the possibility.

"You didn't have to," Eddie said flatly. "I know that as a law enforcement officer investigating the murder, you'd consider anyone associated in any way with the victim a suspect. Especially the creepy and leering mother's boyfriend, which often seems to be the case. At least on those true crime documentaries I've seen."

"Those are often exaggerated for TV drama," Hamilton tried to say, suppressing a chuckle over the all-too-common stereotype. "Real suspects run the gamut," he pointed out. "Depending on the circumstances."

"Be that as it may, I have a rock-solid alibi for the time frame when Juliet went missing and afterward," Eddie maintained. "I was working my shift that night at Carol Creek General. My time card, administrator and patients can verify that."

"So can I," Maureen said supportively. "I called Eddie right after I called you that evening. We video-chatted and I could see that he was at the hospital. He would never have done the awful thing that was done to Juliet and those other women," she stressed.

"Okay, okay," Hamilton said, feeling himself on the defensive but convinced nevertheless of the man's innocence. "You're not a suspect, Eddie," he tried to reassure him. "As it is, the investigation is heating up and we're taking a hard look at others who may be guilty." Or not, he realized.

"All right." Eddie's features relaxed. "We all just want this madness to stop."

"It will." Hamilton felt the pressure of that declaration, knowing the residents of Carol Creek expected nothing less. Nor did he. Or Annette, for that matter. He turned to Maureen and noted that she and Eddie were now holding hands.

"Eddie's asked me to go away with him for the holidays," she said. "His family has a cottage in the Green Mountains of Vermont." Maureen seemed to tighten her grasp of Eddie's hand. "I said yes."

"You did?" Hamilton voiced surprise.

"I need to get out of here for a while," she said. "The memories of what happened to Juliet are just too raw."

"I completely understand," he told her sincerely.

Maureen looked at him. "Really?"

"Of course." Hamilton hated seeing the strain she was under in dealing with the loss of a precious child. If this trip with Eddie could alleviate that, how could he possibly find fault in it? "You should take some time away. It will be good for you."

"Thanks for saying that."

"I mean it, Maureen." Hamilton met her eyes. "I'm glad you've found someone to be with." He glanced at Eddie and back. "You deserve to be happy. Juliet would want that."

"So do you," Maureen uttered, allowing her free hand to rest on his shoulder.

"Actually, since you mention it, I have a date tonight."

Her eyes grew wide with curiosity. "Oh, really. With who?"

"Detective Annette Lynley," Hamilton said proudly. "We've gotten to know each other of late. In fact, I'm making her dinner at the cabin."

Maureen's eyes lit up. "That's wonderful. Detective Lynley is a beautiful woman and an asset to the sheriff's department."

"I agree on both fronts," he said.

"Hope things work out for you two."

"Same with you and Eddie."

"I'll take good care of your sister," Eddie told him.

"Counting on that," Hamilton said, trusting Maureen's judgment and his own that told him this was a positive development. He felt the same way about getting involved with Annette, while looking forward to whatever came their way this evening.

ANNETTE HAD JUST walked into her home after work, anticipating being wined and dined by Hamilton and the potential beyond that, when her cell phone rang for a video chat request from her oldest sibling, Scott. She smiled at the thought of speaking with him, and leaned against the wall in the living room before accepting the call. "Hey, you," she said ardently.

"Hey." Scott grinned at her, his handsome features enhanced by solid gray eyes and black hair that was thick and in a comb-over fade style. An FBI special agent in the Bureau's field office at Louisville, Kentucky, he worked cold case investigations and was married, like their brother Russell. Annette envied both in that respect, while wondering if and when she and their sister, Madison, would tie the knot. "Wanted to make sure you're still on for Christmas," Scott said. "Next up for my pressure tactics is Russell."

Annette chuckled. "We'll both be there," she promised, not feeling as though she could back out now. "So will Madison. Even heard through the grapevine that cousin Gavin plans to show up." Gavin Lynley was a special agent for the Corrections Investigation Division's Special Operations Unit of the Mississippi Department of Corrections, and the next closest thing to a Lynley sibling.

"Seriously?" Scott's eyes widened. "That's news to me."

"Better give him a buzz and confirm his attendance," she suggested.

"I will." He furrowed his brow. "So, what's the latest news on your serial killer investigation?"

Annette brought him up to date on the developments. "With the sheriff's department, the state police and even a couple of your colleagues with the Bureau all working together, we're hoping to stop this before anyone else is killed." She only wondered if that was possible. Especially if the DNA test results on the DeLuca brothers came back negative.

"Yeah, that's always the hope," Scott said. "Unfortunately, sometimes the trail runs cold. That's where I come in."

"You're obviously very good at your job, Scott," she told him, "but our unsub is unlikely to stop what he's doing voluntarily, and this is unlikely to turn into a cold case."

Scott angled his face. "Which is a good thing," he stressed. "The sooner the perp can be flushed out, the better for the investigative team and community."

"I couldn't agree more." Annette imagined that he and Hamilton would get along great and have lots to talk about. She hoped the opportunity presented itself someday. "Well, hate to cut this short, but I have a dinner engagement to get ready for."

"Is that so?" Scott teased her. "Are we dating someone again?"

"I'll let you know," she said simply, recalling the show of support from her family after things had gone sour with her last boyfriend. Annette preferred not to get ahead of herself on where things were headed with Hamilton, not wanting to jinx it.

"Good enough," Scott said without further prying.

Annette smiled. "Tell Paula I said hi." Like Scott, Paula, his wife, was also a member of the law enforcement community.

"Will do."

Upon disconnecting, Annette took a quick shower. Afterward, she blow-dried her hair, then left it down and applied a touch of light fragrance behind her ears and on her wrists, before checking out the wardrobe in her walk-in closet for something suitable to wear on what amounted to a second date with Hamilton. But the first in which they would be at his residence or hers for the outing. Was that a sign that the best was yet to occur between them? Not wanting to overdo it, she went with a nice floral midi dress and black pumps.

When Hamilton arrived, Annette threw on

her single-breasted, belted wrap coat, grabbed her hobo shoulder bag and met him at the door. She hoped to invite him in another time. "Hey."

"Hey." He grinned cutely and gave her an appraisal. "You look nice."

"Thank you." Annette saw that he had ditched the trooper uniform for the first time in her presence, handsome as he looked in it. He had replaced it with a dark wool blazer over a purple herringbone dress shirt, brown khaki pants and tan Chelsea boots. His hair looked freshly washed and his face was smooth-shaven. "You clean up pretty well yourself," she had to say.

He blushed. "I keep some extra clothes at the cabin in case I need them."

They certainly came in handy tonight, Annette thought admiringly. She was sure he was even more striking without the clothing to hide his obviously fit frame. She cut off the light, locked the door and got into his vehicle.

During the drive, Hamilton revealed matter-of-factly, "Maureen and her boyfriend are leaving town for the holidays."

Annette sensed that this had taken him by surprise. "That's a good thing, right?" She assumed it was motivated, at least in part, by Maureen, to escape the pain associated with her daughter's death.

"Yeah, I suppose," he muttered. "I never even

knew she was involved with anyone. Much less seriously enough to share a vacation away from home. Guess it was on a need-to-know basis."

"Are you close enough to your sister that she usually tells you everything going on in her personal and social life?" Annette couldn't help but wonder. She doubted this, based on her own relationship with her adult siblings, their closeness as a family notwithstanding.

"Once upon a time. Not so much in recent years," Hamilton confessed.

"I suspected as much. Maybe with other things going on in her life, Maureen simply waited to tell you when she felt the time was right."

"Yeah," he agreed. "I'm actually happy for her and hope this works out with Eddie, the man in her life. She's had enough disappointments in the relationship department. Maybe this time will be different."

Annette wondered if he was talking about his sister or himself. Perhaps both. "Everyone's allowed to make mistakes along the way where it concerns romance," she put forth. "It's how we learn and grow from it."

Hamilton faced her and said, "You're absolutely right about that. Guess it's something I'm still processing with the mistakes I've made in this regard. Maybe it was easier to project that on my sister and her life, though I wish the very best for her, as always."

"I'm sure she knows that."

"Yeah," he muttered.

Annette smiled, glad to see him own up to his insecurities. It was something that she too was always working at. It gave them something else in common. She looked out the window at the Christmas decorations lighting up homes they passed. She had almost forgotten how beautiful the holiday season could be. Even with the unattractive shadow of a serial killer still on the loose spreading ominously over Carol Creek.

"We're here," Hamilton informed her, moments after they had turned onto Mills Road and pulled into the paved driveway of a rustic, two-story cedar-and-stone cabin.

"Wow," Annette gushed. "When you said you had a lakefront cabin, I wasn't expecting this."

He laughed. "Wait till you see the inside."

"I can hardly wait," she said.

The moment she stepped through the door, which had a Christmas pine wreath on it, Annette wasn't at all disappointed as she took in the spacious layout at a glance. It was an open concept with a high ceiling, hickory hardwood flooring and wicker furniture. A wall of windows with vinyl blinds overlooked Lake Kankiki, and in the living room was a two-story fieldstone fireplace with flames crackling from burning logs. In a corner was a lit and decorated mini-Christmas tree.

"It was the best I could do on short notice," Hamilton said with a grin.

Annette smiled back. "Looks lovely."

"I'll just go check on the food and then give you the grand tour."

"Smells delicious," she told him as the aroma hit her nostrils.

He laughed. "Hope it tastes just as good."

Moments later, while sipping red wine, Annette was shown around the custom kitchen, formal dining room and rec room on the main floor, before they ascended the wooden staircase to the second story.

"It's wonderful," Annette remarked. She couldn't believe he owned this place and wasn't living there year-round.

Hamilton grinned. "If I'd known I would get this reaction, I would've brought you here sooner."

She blushed. "I think this was the perfect time to do so." As it was, they happened to be standing in the primary bedroom suite. It had a large window with a lake vista and rustic furniture, including a vintage sleigh bed.

"Oh, really?" His voice dripped with sexiness. "How perfect?"

She met his desirous eyes. "Perfect enough to take my breath away," she admitted. Or was he managing to do that all by himself?

Holding her gaze, he uttered, "You take my breath away, Annette."

"If I didn't know better, I'd think you were trying to get me into bed, rather than feed me," she said in a deliberately seductive tone.

"And what if I were?" Hamilton questioned, putting his hands on her hips.

"Hmm. I'd wonder about the food burning."

"You needn't wonder any longer. I actually turned off the oven and burners," he said. "I figured our appetites might lie elsewhere for the moment and the food could be heated up afterward."

Annette tasted the wine, knowing full well she wanted him as much as he did her, if not more. "Seems as if you've covered all the bases."

"Not quite." Hamilton grinned hungrily. He took her wineglass and sipped, then set it on the rustic gray dresser. He cupped her cheeks gently and said, "There's still your lips to cover with mine."

"Oh…" She opened her mouth just enough in anticipation for the kiss, which came on cue. It was deep, and made her want much more from him.

Hamilton pulled back. "Not to mention crossing home plate."

Annette suddenly felt hot beneath her clothing. "So, let's not wait any longer to hit a home run."

"I couldn't agree with you more," he responded, taking her into his arms.

Chapter Ten

Hamilton found himself salivating at the prospect of making love to Annette. Yes, he had imagined them having sex from probably the first time he laid eyes on her. But the progress made in actually getting to know the real woman behind the detective would make their being together all the more electrifying. After grabbing a condom from the nightstand, he tossed it onto the cotton chenille bedspread. Then Hamilton began to remove his clothes as he watched Annette do the same. That too turned him on as she slid the dress off, then her underwear, revealing a red-hot body that was toned and taut, with the perfect curves and bends. Long hair hung freely across her shoulders instead of in a restricting updo. Her breasts, medium-sized, were flawlessly rounded, with small, dark nipples. He loved the shape of her long legs and sexiness of her feet, with the small toes proportionate to them.

"You're so beautiful," he had to say, as though this had somehow escaped her notice.

"Look who's talking," she shot back, admiring him as Hamilton stood before her in the nude.

He ate that up, as fitness was an important part of who he was, but was much more in tune with how she turned him on. "I want to make love to you."

"I want that, too," Annette cooed, reaching out to him.

Hamilton scooped her up and they kissed as he carried her to the bed. There, he went to work on making sure she was pleasured from head to toe with his mouth and deft fingers. He wanted to hold back on his own needs till hers had been met, stimulating Annette to her heart's content. Her breath quickened and her body quivered.

"Mmm…" she murmured, clearly giving in to the sensations as a prelude to what would come soon enough. He maintained the intensity of enjoying exploring her till Annette grabbed him and said, "Let's come together—now!"

Hamilton needed no further instructions as his own needs had built up to a frenzy. He quickly ripped open the packet and put on the condom before working his way atop her, where they were a perfect fit for making love. He moved his face down to hers and they kissed passionately as their bodies merged together and their heartbeats synced. *I doubt I ever wanted to be with someone as much as at this moment in time*, Hamilton thought. He willed himself to wait a little longer for Annette to climax, pacing himself with even and sure strokes.

When it happened, she left no doubt that she was ready for him to finish what they started. "I need you to let go, Hamilton," she begged. "I want to go even higher in satisfaction."

"I want that for you, too," he promised. "For both of us."

With that in mind, Hamilton let himself go, plunging into her moist body with a passion that they both craved like nourishment. His own erratic breathing became all but lost with hers as it gave way to the instant in which they reached powerful orgasms simultaneously. Time seemed to stand still with them soaking in the experience while clinging to one another like a second skin.

When it was over and he had rolled off Annette and lay beside her, Hamilton sighed and said as honestly as he could, "That was amazing."

She made a face. "Just amazing?"

"How about incredible and hotter than hot on a cold winter night?"

Annette laughed. "Now, that's more like it."

Hamilton had to laugh himself. "Any way you want to put it, we were great together."

"Yes, we were," she confessed, draping a leg across his.

"It was well worth the wait."

She chuckled. "So, you've been waiting for this to happen, have you?"

His face flushed. "A trooper is allowed to dream, right?"

"Right. And so is a sheriff's detective," she admitted.

He grinned. "Some dreams can actually come true, if you wish hard enough."

"Very true. Speaking of which, I'm dreaming now about being fed by you, having worked up an appetite. Uh, that is why you invited me over, isn't it?"

"Yes. Of course. Food's coming right up." Hamilton stroked her face, having practically forgotten about the mustard-and-brown-sugar-glazed salmon and mashed sweet potatoes he'd prepared, to go with wine. "Sometimes, though, you have to improvise along the way."

Annette giggled. "I'm all for improvising. Maybe later, we can improvise some more."

"Definitely works for me," he responded quickly. "I'm more than willing to go a second round in getting to know each other better intimately. Then moving forward from there."

AN HOUR LATER, they were sitting before the fireplace in wicker egg chairs. Annette couldn't believe just how relaxed she felt in Hamilton's log cabin, following their lovemaking and a tasty meal he'd cooked for her. Where had someone like him been all her life? Surely not anywhere within her viewfinder, if not reach. But he was here now and seemed to like her, if the way they made love like there was no more tomorrow was any indication. And she definitely liked him, too, even if she had no idea where this was headed. What was clear to her was that Hamilton seemed to be everything her last boyfriend was not. That alone was enough to give her a warm feeling inside.

Breaking the quiet introspection between them, Hamilton asked thoughtfully, "So, what are your interests besides law enforcement, education and staying close to your siblings?"

You mean besides you? Annette thought to herself, gazing at the fire. She faced him and responded, "I love to travel, jog, work out at the gym, do crossword puzzles, and watch action-packed and sci-fi movies."

"Interesting." He grinned. "Where have you traveled?"

"The Bahamas, Australia, Hawaii and most of the lower forty-eight states."

"Impressive. Can't say I can match you there, but I've spent some time in the United Kingdom, Sweden, Virgin Islands, and my fair share of states, mainly in the Midwest and Northeastern part of the country."

"Not bad," she told him with a smile. "What are your hobbies?" She imagined with a cabin on the lake, some involved the water.

"In the summer, I love to fish, swim, go scuba diving and boating."

"I kind of figured as much. I enjoy swimming and have been on boats, but not so much the other things."

"I would love to teach you sometime, if you're up for it?"

Annette took that as meaning he wanted to continue to hang out together. "Sure, sounds like it could be fun."

He grinned. "It will be, I promise."

"I'll go along with that." She glanced at the fire, which was still going strong after he had thrown on more logs. "Any nonwater interests?"

"When afforded the time, I like to read spy thrillers," he told her. "And I'm also into watching historical documentaries, comedies and some sci-fi stuff."

"What about all the true crime series on

the air and streaming?" she wondered. "With your knowledge of serial homicides, I would've thought some of these might interest you."

"Not really." Hamilton sat back. "Seems like we're being inundated with true crime material these days. Including in book form. I'd rather stick to what I deal with professionally, in real life."

"Same here," Annette had to agree. She only wished there was less crime for either of them to have to grapple with. Hopefully, once they apprehended the serial killer currently at large in Carol Creek, things might settle down in the new year.

"How do you feel about children?" Hamilton changed the subject in a big way.

Annette batted her eyes at him. "Are you asking if I'd like to have children someday?"

"Yeah. Have you thought about it, one way or the other?"

"Of course." She was glad he'd brought this up. "I'd love to have children, two or three maybe. Coming from a big and loving family, I know how wonderful it can be to have children around, watch them grow up and establish their own lives as part of the process."

He nodded. "I imagine that type of environment would have lent itself to appreciate the joys of family."

"Would you like to have children?" she asked, regarding him curiously. "I know that your own parents weren't around as much as you would have liked, leaving you and Maureen to fend for yourselves. And you stepping in as a surrogate dad for Juliet. But what about being a father to kids of your own?" Since he'd opened the door to this conversation, Annette hoped she wasn't pushing him too far.

"I'm open to having kids," he told her matter-of-factly. "If I have the right partner, I see no reason why we couldn't start a family and do better at it than my own parents, while learning from the time I spent with Juliet and how I might have done more in being there for her."

"Good." Annette flashed him a brilliant smile, glad that he was trying to turn Juliet's tragedy into a positive for his own life as a potential father. *I feel as though we're on the same page in being open to becoming parents and the steps leading up to that*, Annette thought. Maybe this was a sign that they were on to something in becoming involved with one another. Or was she seeing things through rose-colored glasses?

"How do you feel about heading back upstairs?" Hamilton asked in earnest.

Annette recalled the sexual talk about improvising when in bed before. "I say let's do it," she stated bluntly, the thought of making love to him again causing a tingle inside her.

He grinned. "I was hoping you'd agree."

Hamilton stood and took Annette's hand, helping her to her feet. They began to kiss and cuddle. By the time they made it to his bedroom, Annette was pretty worked up in wanting to be with him. Only this time, she would be the aggressor, wanting to please him and prolong the action.

After engaging in foreplay that left them both panting and purring, Annette climbed atop Hamilton's rock-hard body. While he caressed her breasts, she guided herself onto him and they let themselves enjoy the experience as they made love. When the climaxes came, Annette locked lustful eyes with Hamilton, arched her back and succumbed to the satisfaction they brought to each other. In the waning moments of passion, she fell upon him and brought their mouths together, enjoying his taste and closeness.

When it was over, Annette fell asleep on Hamilton's chest, and they spent the night together.

Startled awake the following morning by a cell phone ringing, Annette realized it was hers. She slid out of Hamilton's arms, naked, and rolled off the bed. Lifting the phone out of her hobo bag, Annette saw that the caller was forensic scientist Kelly Okamoto of the ISP Fort Wayne Regional Lab's Forensic Biology Section.

"Hey, Kelly," she said in an easygoing voice with the phone to her ear, as she saw Hamilton stirring awake.

"Detective Lynley, I just wanted you to know that we took the DNA collected from Patrick and Paul DeLuca and compared it to the unknown profile extracted from the strand of hair removed from Juliet's mouth."

Annette was tense as she watched Hamilton sit up, sleepy-eyed but alert. "And what did you learn?" she asked the forensic analyst, hoping they might be able to break the case wide-open with one brother, if not the other.

"Neither of the DeLuca brothers was a match for the unidentified DNA profile," Kelly answered. "Sorry to have to tell you that the hair strand belongs to someone else."

"Thanks, Kelly," Annette told her disappointedly, and hung up.

"What did you find out?" Hamilton asked interestedly, gazing at her.

Frowning, while ignoring that she was completely exposed to him outside the bed, Annette responded bleakly, "We didn't get a match. The unsub is still unknown and remains at large."

HAMILTON WAS ON PATROL, having reconciled himself to the fact that neither Patrick nor Paul DeLuca was the Christmas Lights Killer. As it was, he hadn't really expected a match, considering the brothers had voluntarily given up their DNA. Not a likely scenario for anyone guilty of being a serial killer. But it had been worth a try anyway, considering that the DeLucas did own a vehicle with tires that matched the tire tread evidence near the crime scene that also happened to be just outside the Christmas tree farm owned by the DeLuca brothers.

So we keep trying till the unsub is revealed and caught, Hamilton told himself while driving. His thoughts turned to Annette, giving him a sexual tickle. He was still riding high after the earth-shattering sex they'd had twice yesterday. She had managed to keep pace with him every step of the way and beyond. Or was it the other way around? Whatever the case, she was the real deal as far as he was concerned and he wanted to pursue something with her. He believed she wanted this, too, and they could work toward that once the holidays were behind them and her visit with family. His own family, or Maureen, would be in Vermont. Meaning, he was very likely going to have to spend Christmas alone. Hamilton didn't cherish the thought, but would try not to think about it too much while he kept himself occupied with work.

When a call came in informing him that a car driven by a male murder suspect was speeding erratically through his district, Hamilton joined in the chase of the alleged perpetrator. He pressed down on the accelerator, racing through the streets, till he spotted the brown Buick Encore GX Essence. Tailing it was a white Dodge Charger Pursuit. Hamilton recognized the driver as ISP Trooper Al Hernandez. The forty-five-year-old veteran was a friend, married for the second time, and had four children.

As Hamilton attempted to cut off the suspect, he managed to dart off in a different direction. Hernandez stayed close to him, with another trooper vehicle entering the picture in hot pursuit. Hamilton veered right and headed down another street, sure that he could beat the suspect before he could enter a main street that would allow him to blend in more easily with other traffic, complicating efforts to stop him. *You're not going to get away that easily*, Hamilton thought, gripping the steering wheel tightly as he maneuvered past other vehicles and spotted the Buick barreling toward him.

Suddenly, Hamilton heard the sound of gunfire and then felt his car being hit by a bullet. Then another. He quickly realized that the suspect had slid a semiautomatic weapon out of the window, desperately hoping to shoot his way out of the predicament he was in. Fortunately, the shot missed Hamilton, but was close enough to get his attention. He realized that a bulletproof vest would only go so far in staying alive. Which he fully intended to do.

Just as he removed his own firearm and was prepared to fire back, the suspect's vehicle was rammed from behind by Hernandez. The impact and the high speed at which the perp was traveling forced him to lose control of his car. It flipped twice, ending upside down. The trooper vehicles quickly surrounded it. Hamilton exited his car, weapon drawn.

Trooper Al Hernandez also got out of his vehicle. Thickly built and around Hamilton's height, he was brown-eyed and, beneath his campaign hat, had brown hair trimmed in a short, textured cut. "You okay?" he asked.

"Still in one piece," Hamilton told him thankfully. "Good thing he was a bad shot."

"Yeah. That's for sure."

"My car may need some repair work, though."

"That's one way to get an upgrade," Hernandez joked.

They both turned to the suspect, who appeared unconscious and injured. He looked to be in his midtwenties, was on the lean side, and had two-toned hair in a blowout style and a dark gunslinger beard and moustache. Once it was determined that he was no longer a threat, the suspect was removed from the vehicle, at which time he began to stir. A quick check of his vital signs told Hamilton that his injuries were not serious but he still needed medical attention. After the man was placed under arrest, an ambulance arrived to transport him to the hospital.

Later, the suspect was identified as twenty-four-year-old Richard Kruger, who lived in Fort Wayne and was the registered owner of the Buick Encore. He was charged with the murder of his live-in girlfriend, Mandy Langham, evading police and resisting arrest, reckless endangerment, and possession of drugs.

Hamilton chalked the experience up to all in a day's work as a state trooper. Still, he longed to be able to move into the ISP's Special Investigations Section, where he could better tap into his skills and insight concerning criminal elements. He had just left the auto repair shop where his vehicle was being worked on for two bullet holes, when Hamilton received a text message from Annette. It said disturbingly,

Another woman has gone missing.

Chapter Eleven

When Annette received word that Lucy Bee-cham, a thirty-one-year-old assistant general manager for an advertising agency, had failed to show up for work that morning, alarm bells went off in her head. She had even texted Hamilton about it because she suspected it could be related to their current investigation. Though it may have been jumping the gun to assume the worst-case scenario, the report that another local woman was missing at all was more than enough to get her attention in the face of a ruthless serial killer at large.

Following up on this, Annette drove to McKinnon Marketing on Fuller Avenue, where she met with Heida McKinnon, the chief executive officer.

"Thanks for taking this seriously, Detective Lynley," Heida said, as they sat in twill fabric chairs in her spacious office. "I'm really worried about Lucy."

"We take all cases of missing persons seriously," Annette asserted, gazing at the slender woman who was in her forties and had crimson hair in uneven layers and green eyes behind browline glasses. *Especially those that fit certain characteristics hard to ignore*, she thought. "Can you tell me what gives you cause for concern in this instance?"

"Mainly it's because Lucy was supposed to be here at eight a.m. for a presentation." Heida took a breath. "Well, she never showed up."

"Perhaps she overslept," Annette suggested. "Or got the time mixed up?"

"If you knew Lucy, you'd know she took her job very seriously," Heida stated. "She wasn't the type to oversleep. Or have a mix-up on the time. The fact that she still isn't here after ten o'clock tells me something must have happened to her."

Annette had no reason not to believe this was unusual behavior for the assistant general manager. But as a detective, she still needed to cover the possibility that Lucy was missing of her own accord. "Have you tried calling her?"

"Of course," Heida snapped. "Several times. Went straight to voice mail."

"Hmm, that is strange," Annette admitted. "Does she have a husband or partner you could check with on her whereabouts?"

"Lucy is married to her work." Heida sat back. "She's been single and unattached for as long as I've known her. I never asked why, but suspect that she had a bad breakup years ago and didn't want to risk going through that again."

I certainty can relate to that, Annette thought, having gone down that road. But Hamilton had given her good reason to believe that not all hope was lost when it came to finding romance again. Could this have been the case for Lucy, too, without her colleagues being privy to it? "Do you know if Ms. Beecham has had any concerns about her safety? Maybe a stalker or—"

"Yes," Heida broke in, "Lucy did express some fears about a custodial worker, Ross Keach, who kept hitting on her and didn't seem to want to take no for an answer. Out of an abundance of caution for any of our employees feeling threatened, we let him go last month."

Annette took note of this. "Did she talk about having any negative experiences with him after that?"

"Not to me. But she could have decided to keep it to herself at that point."

"Do you have a recent picture of Ms. Beecham?"

"Yes. There's one on my cell phone that we took at the firm's Christmas party two weeks ago," Heida answered, and grabbed the phone from the pocket of her blue jacket and pulled up the photograph.

Annette gazed at the image. Lucy was small and attractive with blue eyes on a round face and long, curly blond hair with blunt bangs. "Can you send this to my cell phone?"

"Yes."

Once she received the picture, Annette rose. "I'll need Ms. Beecham's address and the type of car she drives."

Heida gave the address and said, "Lucy has a Lexus LS 500."

Noting this, Annette told her, "We'll check and see if she's home. If not, we'll consider Lucy Beecham officially missing and investigate further."

Heida furrowed her brow. "Hope you find her and she's okay."

"I hope so, too," Annette told her sincerely.

"With what's been going on lately with a serial killer out there, all kinds of horrible things go through your mind," she admitted.

Don't I know it, Annette told herself realistically. But she still wanted to keep an open mind on the disappearance. "Let's just wait and see," she voiced tonelessly, while decidedly darker thoughts danced in her head.

ANNETTE WENT WITH Will to the home of Lucy Beecham on York Street. The single-story custom dwelling was in a cul-de-sac and had decorations up. A car was in the driveway. "Not exactly a Lexus LS 500," Will commented.

"True," Annette agreed, eyeing the red Kia Rio. "Wonder who it belongs to?" She recalled that Heida implied that Lucy lived alone. If so, could an intruder—or even a killer—be inside the house, perhaps burglarizing it? Would someone be so bold as to commit such a crime in broad daylight with the getaway car in full view of neighbors?

"We'd better find out." They went up to the door and knocked, while Will yelled, "This is the police!"

Annette heard a dog bark and what sounded like footsteps. She kept a hand close to the firearm tucked in her outside-the-waistband holster. The door opened and a slender teenage girl with brown eyes stood there, looking shocked to see them. She ran a hand through long, straight brunette hair with blue highlights and asked nervously, "What's going on?"

"Maybe you could tell us," Annette said cautiously. "I'm Detective Lynley and this is Detective Hossack. What's your name?"

"Peyton Cortese."

"Is there anyone else inside?" Will questioned.

"No, just me." She seemed to think about it and added, "Oh, and Lucy's dog, Jetson."

"Actually, we're here to see Lucy Beecham," Annette told the girl, sensing that she was not a threat. "Is she home?"

"No," Peyton replied casually. "Guess Lucy's at work about now."

Will peered at her. "Who are you, exactly?"

"I'm her neighbor. I live in that house over there."

Annette followed the path of her thin finger, which pointed at another house two over in the cul-de-sac, also decorated for the holidays, with a Nissan Rogue and a Jeep Gladiator Mojave parked in the driveway. She turned back to the teenager and asked suspiciously, "Is that your Kia in the driveway?"

"Yeah," the girl admitted. "My parents gave it to me earlier this year for my sixteenth birthday."

Annette still wasn't quite convinced the girl was on the level and not a thief or whatever and asked wryly, "Do you always drive your car such a short distance between houses?"

Peyton giggled. "I'm going to visit a friend after I'm done here," she explained.

"Why are you at Lucy Beecham's house?" Will demanded.

The girl ran a hand through her hair again.

"Because of her busy schedule, Lucy pays me to take Jetson out for a walk when she's not around and I also water her plants when she's out of town. I was about to take Jetson out when you guys showed up." Her eyes narrowed uneasily. "So, why are you looking for Lucy anyway?"

Annette weighed how much she should divulge, then realized they needed to be forthcoming if they wanted her help. "Lucy's been reported missing."

"What?" Peyton's lower lip quivered.

"She never showed up at work this morning," Annette said. "Which was cause for alarm."

"Mind if we take a look around inside?" Will asked the girl. "Might give us a clue as to her whereabouts."

Including the possibility, remote as it seemed, that the missing woman could be inside her own house and unable to communicate, Annette thought.

"Go ahead," Peyton gave her permission to enter. "Hope nothing bad has happened to Lucy."

"So do we," Annette uttered, and they went inside. Almost immediately, an Australian shepherd raced toward them, seemingly curious about the unexpected company, and jumped playfully on Annette. Annette scratched him under the chin, which seemed to agree with

Jetson. She was reminded of the pets she had growing up in Oklahoma. Maybe once she had a family of her own, she could get another dog.

After Will played with Jetson a bit, Peyton got the dog to come to her. She put him on a leash and said, "I'm just going to take him out to do his thing now. I suppose it'll be okay to leave you in here alone."

"We won't damage or take anything," Annette promised. Unless it was called for in the course of the investigation into the disappearance of the assistant general manager. "We just need to find her," she said with a sense of urgency. Peyton nodded and went outside with the dog.

"Let's see if Beecham left any clues about where she might be," Will said. "Or who she could be with."

"All right." Annette took a sweeping glance at the layout, which was an airy, open concept, and the art deco furniture. The house looked clean, and she noted that there were no dirty dishes in the kitchen. In fact, nothing seemed out of place, even with a dog, impressing her. "I'll go check out Lucy's bedroom." She headed down a hall, passing two smaller rooms in favor of the primary bedroom. The first thing Annette noticed right off the bat was that the four-poster bed with its crinkle comforter was made up, as though it had not been slept in overnight. *I never make my bed in the morning*, she thought, as it was the last thing on her mind in needing to get ready for work and grab a bite to eat, before heading out the door. This suggested to her that Lucy may not have gone to bed last night, if she made it home at all after work. *I'm guessing, though, that as clearly a neat freak, she would've made the bed before leaving this morning had Lucy been there*, Annette told herself. Instincts made her feel otherwise in believing that the missing woman had either met up with someone voluntarily, or was lured somewhere by someone. Either way Annette sliced it, this was troubling as far as Lucy's prospects for safety were concerned.

After taking a cursory look around the room with the same art deco furnishings as elsewhere, and seeing nothing that caused suspicion, Annette met Will in the living room and asked, "Did you find anything?"

"Yeah." Wearing a latex glove, he held up a notepad. "This was on the desk in her home office. It says that she was meeting a client at eight last night."

"Hmm…" Annette took a closer look at the note. It didn't mention the client by name or gender. Or where this meeting was supposed to take place.

"What do you think?"

"Honestly, I think that it deepens the mystery of her disappearance. Either Lucy's meeting with this client was more personal than professional and time got away from her or she was being led into a trap."

Will's brow furrowed. "We need to find out which way this goes."

Annette was in complete agreement as her cell phone buzzed. She took it out of the pocket of her flare-leg pants and saw that the caller was Reserve Deputy Shelton Kuen. "Lynley," she answered in an even tone.

"Lucy Beecham's car has been located," Shelton said.

"Where?" Annette asked.

"Just off Boers Creek Road. Near the railroad tracks."

That's not far from here, she mused. "Any sign of Lucy?"

"Not yet," he replied. "The car was empty. We're still checking out the area."

"We're on our way," Annette said, and hung up.

"What is it?" Will looked at her.

"Lucy Beecham's vehicle was found, but no sign of her." They exchanged glances and Annette knew both were wondering the same thing.

Would the missing woman be found dead in the trunk of her car, similar to Juliet McCade?

"Let's go," Will said.

Annette bobbed her head, having a feeling that this would end badly.

HAMILTON HAD GOTTEN word that the gray Lexus LS 500 driven by the missing woman named Lucy Beecham had been located near Boers Creek Road. He took a shortcut to get there, wanting to see for himself if this latest disappearance was the real deal. Or perfectly explainable without the presence of foul play being involved. The timing of this concerned him. None of them wanted to see another female victim of a demented serial killer. Yet this was obviously what was going through the minds of everyone involved in the investigation.

All we can do is hope that Lucy Beecham is safe and sound, in spite of her apparently abandoned car, Hamilton thought, as he pulled behind a squad car. Further up, Annette and Will emerged from another vehicle and were approaching the Lexus, which was parked just short of the railroad tracks. Hamilton got out of his car and caught up to Annette. "Hey," he spoke routinely, as if they were still merely law enforcement colleagues and not lovers.

"Hey." She met his eyes briefly, then gazed toward the railroad tracks. "There's still no word on Lucy Beecham's whereabouts."

"Have they checked the trunk?" he hated to ask, with fresh memories of Juliet left in the trunk of her car.

"About to do so right now," she responded uneasily, and they walked over to the missing woman's vehicle. Will was conferring with Reserve Deputy Shelton Kuen, who was big-boned, brown-eyed, and had a bald fade haircut, black in color.

Shelton acknowledged them and said, "I was just telling Detective Hossack that it appears as if the car was left here overnight. A passerby named Florence Oshiro spotted the vehicle this morning, thought it looked suspicious, and called 911."

"Let's get the trunk open," Annette ordered, and Hamilton wondered if it could be done the easy way or the hard way.

As if reading his mind, Shelton said, "The car was left unlocked." He put on nitrile gloves and opened the driver's-side door, whereby he found the trunk release lever and pushed it to open the trunk.

Hamilton could feel the hairs stand on the back of his neck while slowly lifting the trunk lid up with a gloved hand, expecting to find a body. But the trunk was empty, giving him a sigh of relief.

"She's not here," Annette said, a ray of hope in her voice that Lucy Beecham might still be alive.

"So, where is she?" Hamilton asked, as reality set in —the missing woman's car left unattended with no communication from her was still a bad sign.

"Maybe she had car trouble and hitched a ride," Shelton suggested.

Will took out his cell phone and held it up. "There's reception, meaning that she would have called for help if there was a problem with her car."

"According to her boss, Lucy wasn't picking up her phone at all this morning," Annette said. "Which tells me she was unable to do so, for one reason or another." She interrupted herself when her cell phone rang.

Hamilton listened as she answered and said a few terse words to the caller. The expression on Annette's face seemed to go from optimistic to downright depressed in one fell swoop, before she hung up. "What?" he almost dreaded to ask.

"A body has been found in a wooded area about a quarter of a mile from here off Lakewood Road," she stated bleakly. "It's believed to be Lucy Beecham."

Chapter Twelve

"I hate that this has turned into another nightmare," Detective Charisma Robinson said morosely as she greeted Annette and the other law enforcement personnel to arrive at the scene.

"You and me both." Annette grimaced, meeting the blue eyes of the thirty-five-year-old expectant mother with platinum blond hair in a short shag. She had hoped against hope that there would be a different outcome, but seeing the victim was believing that, in fact, Lucy Beecham was dead. Annette eyed the advertising professional as she lay on her stomach in a wooded area and sparsely populated section of Carol Creek. It was less than two miles from Lucy's house. Wrapped around her neck and long blond hair like a scarf were Christmas string lights. She was fully clothed in a navy wool crepe blazer, black straight-leg trouser pants and black leather dress booties. Some of her personal belongings were scattered nearby, as if no longer of consequence to the person responsible for her death.

"Looks like she may have been trying to get away from her assailant," Hamilton deduced.

Annette could see from the dirt and snow on her clothing and positioning of the body that Lucy did appear as though she had been dropped and attempted to crawl or stumble away before the unsub caught up to her and finished what he had started. "I think you're right," Annette told him. "Only the killer was not about to let that happen."

"Which fits the pattern of the other poor women who crossed paths with the Christmas Lights Killer," Charisma remarked. Her words led Annette to muse about Juliet. She could see from Hamilton's expression that his niece's murder had resurfaced in his mind, although it probably never stayed away for long.

"Any idea how the victim might have run into the unsub?" he asked and muttered something under his breath.

"It appears as though she was planning to meet an unnamed client last night," Will said. "Whether or not she ever did is anyone's guess. But this would be a definite person of interest."

"There was also a former custodial worker at Lucy's place of employment whom she accused of harassing her, leading to his firing," Annette pointed out. "He could have wanted revenge as part of the serial murders he was perpetrating."

"Those suspects are a good place to start," Hamilton said, glancing at the victim and back. "Whether either pans out remains to be seen."

"We won't know till we know," she told him, wanting to get the unsub so badly she couldn't stand it. She knew Hamilton was of the same mind, if primarily in memory of his niece.

"Very true," he said, giving her an unreadable look that had Annette remembering their night of passion, even as the gravity of the current situation weighed heavily on her.

Annette gathered everyone and said, "Though somewhat remote, we need to canvass the area for any possible witnesses, surveillance video, etc."

"I'll jump right on that," Charisma said, and others concurred.

When Josephine Washburn, county coroner and medical examiner, arrived, Annette waited to see her take on the latest casualty to rock Carol Creek.

Frowning, Josephine complained, "Looks like the grinch is dead set on ruining everyone's holidays."

"Tell me about it." Annette tsked, glancing at Hamilton and back. "Have you met Trooper Hamilton McCade?"

"We've crossed paths once or twice." Josephine gazed at him. "Trooper McCade."

"Dr. Washburn," he said knowingly.

"I'm sorry about your niece," she acknowledged.

He gave a silent nod.

Annette broke the awkwardness of the moment by shifting the focus to the present death, when she pointed toward the wooded spot where Lucy Beecham lay dead. "She's over there..."

"Let's have a look," the ME uttered, as she slipped on her latex gloves while visually inspecting the decedent. Then she did a preliminary exam before saying tonelessly, "The cause of death was almost certainly ligature strangulation, with the ligature being the string Christmas lights wrapped around the victim's neck. So, yes, we are talking about a homicide here, as if you had any doubts to the contrary."

"We didn't," Annette had to say bleakly. "The MO and manner of death fit the pattern of the serial killer we're searching for."

"Better find him soon," Josephine warned. "Not sure how many more of these strangulation deaths I can take."

"We're on the same page there," Will told her. "What's the estimated time of death?"

Josephine studied the victim further and said, "Based on a few things, I would have to say she has been dead for at least twelve hours. Maybe more. I'll see if I can narrow that down even more after completing the autopsy."

Annette only needed to do some quick arithmetic to estimate that Lucy was probably killed somewhere between eight last night, when she was supposed to meet with a client, and midnight. Could she have been kidnapped and held for a while before being murdered?

"What do we have here?" Josephine lifted one of Lucy's hands and carefully removed from it what appeared to be a strand of hair. "I'm guessing the victim managed to grab ahold of this during the struggle for survival."

Hamilton winced. "When it's compared with the hair strand found with Juliet, I'm sure we'll find that the unsub is one and the same."

Annette had to agree, having no reason to believe they were dealing with a copycat killer. "If so, we'll still need to connect it to someone we can identify by name and place." Meaning that the DNA profile was a key piece of evidence, but was only one step toward piecing the puzzle of serial murder together.

"First things first," Josephine told them, placing the hair in an evidence bag. "This will need to be processed and you can go from there."

"We found something else promising to add to the discussion," Loretta Covington, the crime

scene analyst, said as she approached the group.
"A tire track was discovered just up the road that
looks an awful lot like the Goodyear Wrangler
Fortitude HT track found near the crime scene
of Juliet McCade's murder."

"Really?" Hamilton hoisted a brow with interest. "Let's take a look."

Annette walked between him and Will, with
Loretta leading the way, before they came to an
area where the street merged with a dirt path
that had only a dusting of snow. The partial tire
track was clear as day as CSIs protected the potential crime scene from being corrupted. All
Annette could think of was that a match here
would be further proof that they were dealing
with the same unsub, bringing them closer to
identifying him. "We need a cast of the tire
track," she ordered.

"You've got it," Loretta declared, and pro-
ceeded accordingly.

A little later, after updating Sheriff Teixeira
on the latest homicide and where things currently stood in the investigation, Annette returned to her office. Hamilton was waiting for
her, sitting with his long legs stretched out. She
fought to ignore the sexual vibes he exuded by
his very presence, along with the images that
sprang up in her mind from their recent history. "Sorry," she said. "Took a bit longer than

I thought with the give-and-take between me and the sheriff."

"No problem," Hamilton told her. "I understand how much pressure you're under with this case. Every other homicide associated with it only makes the situation more intense and frustrating."

"Exactly." Annette was sure he could relate to one degree or another. "Fortunately, Sheriff Teixeira is allowing us to stay the course till we see this through." She sat at her desk, which separated them, even when she wanted only to fall into his arms. "So, how was your day?" she asked him casually.

Hamilton frowned. "Don't ask."

"Now you've got me curious," Annette admitted. "I'm asking."

He sat back. "Well, I started off the day pursuing a murder suspect and getting shot at in the process."

"Seriously?" Her brows knitted with worry. "Are you okay?"

"Yeah, I'm good. He managed to put a couple of holes in my squad car. Other than that, I escaped unscathed."

"Thank goodness." The idea of serious harm coming to Hamilton was something Annette didn't even want to imagine, feeling as close to him as she was starting to. "So, what happened to the suspect?"

"He flipped his car, sustained minor injuries and faces a slew of charges," Hamilton told her. "Not the least of which is the stabbing murder of his girlfriend."

"Wow." Annette wrinkled her nose. "A tough day for you."

"Not as tough as yours," he said matter-of-factly.

"That's debatable," she countered. "Murder is murder, with consequences for those left behind."

"True enough." Hamilton set his jaw. "Hope Lucy Beecham's murder can give us the answers we need to bring the culprit to justice and let the chips fall where they may as far as lingering consequences."

"We'll see what the crime lab comes up with interview suspects, and see where those chips fall," Annette agreed.

Hamilton shifted in the chair. "I need to talk to Maureen before she hears about the latest murder and freaks out again about losing Juliet."

"I think your sister is stronger than you give her credit for, Hamilton. Maybe you need to just trust that Maureen is doing what she can to move on, even if bad things are still happening out there."

He nodded. "I'm sure you're right on both scores. I just need to hear that from her and then I'll leave it alone."

"That sounds fair," Annette said, knowing full well that her siblings had a tendency as well to be overprotective. She was probably just as guilty in reverse. She liked the idea of having someone in her life who would be just as keen in always being there in her times of need. Someone like Hamilton.

COMING ON THE heels of Juliet's murder, the news that another local female had lost her life to the serial killer wasn't something that Hamilton wanted to share with Maureen. But there was no sugarcoating the truth. Or hiding from it. He was sure, as Annette had suggested, that Maureen was thick-skinned enough to be able to deal with such news without falling apart. She understood that they were working overtime to catch the perp, but even that wasn't always enough to stop crafty killers from killing again and again.

Still, she deserved better, Hamilton believed as he headed to Maureen's house. So did the other families left to grieve the crimes committed by the Christmas Lights Killer. And others like him. Justice would prevail ultimately. Of that, he was certain. It usually did in such cases. Yet it couldn't come soon enough.

Hamilton felt solace that Annette had come into his life at seemingly just the right time. She was the type of distraction that any man could warm up to. Only, the sheriff's detective was becoming much more than a distraction to him. He could actually envision a future with her. Was this what she wanted? Would her family approve of him as another person in law enforcement, encroaching on one of their own?

At least Maureen has my back where it concerns seeing Annette, Hamilton told himself, pulling into the driveway. The least he could do was have hers in the same way as his sister tried to give romance another shot with Eddie.

The moment Hamilton walked through the door, Maureen gave him a hug and said, "I know that another woman has been killed."

He frowned. "Doesn't take long for news to travel in Carol Creek."

"Or anywhere, for that matter," she told him. "Especially of this magnitude."

"We have some strong leads on the killer," he said, hoping this would give her a little satisfaction that they were on the right trail.

Maureen stared at him. "Juliet is gone now and nothing will ever bring my daughter back," she emphasized. "The man responsible for her death will get his, one way or another. Don't let it overwhelm you so you lose sight of what's most important."

He held her gaze. "Which is?" What could be more important than family?

"Being happy in life for as long as you can, never knowing what's around the corner. I honestly felt that Mom and Dad wanted that for us, even if they weren't very good at articulating their feelings."

"You really think so?"

"Yes," she replied firmly. "I wanted it for Juliet, too, and she lived up to that for the most part. Now I want it for you. And me as well."

"Same here." He grinned at her, their lives from childhood to now flashing before his eyes. "So, when do you and Eddie leave for the Green Mountains of Vermont?"

"Tomorrow," Maureen told him. "Between workplace stresses and everything else, I'm really looking forward to this time away to relax and get my head straight."

"I want that for you, too, more than you know," Hamilton said. "Even afterward, hopefully you and Eddie will have more getaways in your future."

"I hope so." She tilted her face and smiled. "Maybe some getaways are in your future as well, now that a certain detective has entered the picture."

He couldn't help but smile at the notion. "We'll see how it goes."

In his mind, Hamilton was already thinking in those terms, while contemplating just what it would take to make Annette all his.

ANNETTE CARRIED HER work home with her that night. She pored over what they knew and didn't know at this point pertaining to the Christmas Lights Killer. Yes, there were still leads to follow on the latest murder attributed to the killer. But the fact that this killer was ruthless and handpicking his victims whenever the spirit moved him told her that they needed to step up their efforts even more. So, where was he now? What exactly was making him tick, aside from the thrill of the kill? Had Lucy Beecham simply been in the wrong place at the wrong time? Or had she been set up to die by someone who had a beef against her?

By the time she called it a night, Annette had allowed those disturbing thoughts to settle down. Hamilton suddenly occupied her mind. The idea that he could have been shot that very day frightened her. She didn't want to lose him to senseless violence. But did she actually even have him? Yes, they had made passionate love together and seemed to hit it off in most areas. Yet he still hadn't fully opened up to her. After all, the man hadn't even invited her to his main house. Why not? Was that somehow off-limits?

Annette tossed those thoughts back at herself. She hadn't exactly welcomed Hamilton inside her house with open arms. So, was she any less guilty in being cautious about not wanting to move too quickly in this relationship if they could even call it one? Maybe she would invite him over for dinner tomorrow. After all, it was her turn to do the cooking. She was open to whatever might happen thereafter.

Chapter Thirteen

Hamilton was sent a copy of the autopsy report on Lucy Beecham, believed to be the latest victim of the Christmas Lights Killer. As he suspected, the assistant general manager of an ad agency had died due to ligature strangulation. Or throttling from a string of Christmas lights. The medical examiner had declared the death to be a homicide. This brought back fresh images in Hamilton's head of what it must have been like for Juliet in her final moments before she stopped breathing. He could only hope that she lost consciousness as soon as possible and had been somehow able to conjure up good thoughts to separate from the horror of the moment.

Driving to the ISP Fort Wayne Regional Laboratory, Hamilton wanted to see firsthand if the crime scene evidence collected in the Beecham homicide was a match for that obtained in Juliet's death, confirming that they were dealing with the same unsub. In the Forensic Biology Section, he got right to it with forensic scientist Kelly Okamoto. "What did you make of the latest hair sample collected?" he asked her.

Kelly scratched her cheek and replied calmly, "Well, the DNA analysis makes it clear that the hair definitely came from a white male." She had a magnified image of the hair on her monitor.

Hamilton reacted. "And how does it compare to the previous strand of hair analyzed?"

"The DNA profile was an exact match between the two strands of hair," she answered. She brought up the hair samples, side by side, on the screen. "Or, in other words, both belonged to the same individual."

So the same killer did perpetrate both attacks, Hamilton mused, peering at the hair strands from two different homicides. And likely, because of the common MO, also responsible for the other related murders committed with Christmas lights. "Any chance that the most recent forensic unknown profile collected might somehow magically show up in the database?" he wondered, realizing this was a longshot at best.

"Sorry." Kelly wrinkled her nose. "We put the second DNA profile in the state database and National DNA Index System and got the same result. There was no match to any arrestee or convicted offender."

"Figured as much," Hamilton voiced disappointedly, "but it was worth a try."

"Always," she concurred. "But the good news is we now know for sure that you're dealing with the same unsub here. And if he ever is arrested, we'll be able to collect his DNA and link him to these murders."

"Yeah." Hamilton sighed. "With any luck, though, we'll be able to nab him before he can get to another victim."

"Of course," Kelly said. "At least the unsub has given us something to work with, even if he's trying to conceal his guilt."

"That can only last so long." But it could still be long enough for the unsub to continue his killing ways.

In the Microanalysis Unit, Hamilton found Bernard Levinson, the forensic analyst who had been tasked with comparing the tire tread castings made from tracks left near two crime scenes. "So, what are we looking at with the latest cast of the tire track?" Hamilton asked urgently.

Touching his glasses while sitting at his workstation, Bernard responded, "I'd have to say that the tire tread looks virtually identical to the Goodyear all-season, all-terrain tread from the first cast."

Hamilton chewed on his lower lip. "Hmm… Can you show me on your monitor?"

"Yeah, sure." Bernard pulled both castings up, side by side. "Though there is less of the tire track in the second casting, you can see enough of it to compare with the first one to see the similarities in the tread."

"You're right," Hamilton agreed. They did appear to come from the same type of tire. But he still needed further confirmation.

"You should check with that tire center again to be sure," Bernard said, reading his mind.

"I will," he told him. "But at the moment, I'll assume these tracks probably came from the same vehicle."

"Looks that way."

Hamilton left the crime laboratory and drove over to the tire center, where Pete Lipton, the manager, studied the cast of the partial tire track found near Lucy Beecham's body and asserted, "Like the other tire track you showed me, this is also a tread from a Goodyear Wrangler Fortitude HT."

"Really?" Hamilton believed him, but put just enough doubt in his inflection that, as anticipated, Pete once again double-checked with his top mechanic, Clayton Serricchio, who reached the same conclusion.

"I'm sure you've narrowed down the vehicles in the local area that use these tires," Pete told Hamilton.

"We have," he acknowledged. "Unfortunately, we're still searching for the vehicle in question." And in the process, the unsub driving it while on the hunt for more potential victims.

After getting back on the road, Hamilton headed for Carol Creek, wondering if Annette and Will had made any meaningful break-throughs on the case. Beyond that, he thought about the progress made between him and Annette on a personal level and just how far it could go, if both were willing.

WHILE DRIVING, Annette pondered the findings from the medical examiner, and the ISP crime lab's Forensic Biology Section and Microanalysis Unit, that linked the deaths of Lucy Beecham and Juliet McCade. It was chilling, to say the least, when put together like a whodunit mystery that was anything but fiction, the fragments of a deadly puzzle.

We're talking about the same unsub strangling to death attractive women, Annette told herself, as though there was any doubt of that in her mind, with the evidence only confirming this, more or less. The Christmas Lights Killer was preying on those he happened upon or were chosen by design and camouflaged as random. Either way, it wasn't good and incumbent upon them to bring the killer's murder and mayhem to a grinding halt.

She was on her way to see Virgil Flynn, a businessman whom Lucy had been scheduled to meet the night she died, according to Lucy's employer, Heida McKinnon. Had this meeting taken place, only with tragic results? Annette parked in the lot of the Flynn Real Estate Agency on Prairie Street and stepped outside. Though the air was chilly, the snow had mostly disappeared from the streets and sidewalks, while still clinging to rooftops and tree limbs.

She went inside and spotted a slender Hispanic woman in her thirties with brown hair in a short bob, sitting at a desk while talking on the phone. Turning in the other direction, Annette was met by a man of medium build in his sixties with blue eyes and a gray horseshoe haircut. "Detective Lynley, I presume?" he asked.

"Yes," she told him, meeting his gaze.

"Virgil Flynn. Heida told me you would be dropping by to talk about Lucy Beecham. Why don't we step over to my desk?"

"All right." Annette followed him to a corner

of the large office, where there was a double pedestal executive desk. He offered her a seat on a padded armchair and sat himself behind the desk on a faux leather chair with flip arms.

Virgil interlocked thick fingers and said, "First of all, I feel terrible about what happened to Lucy. But I had nothing to do with her death."

Annette peered at him. "I understand that Ms. Beecham had an appointment to meet you at eight the night before last," she said. "What was the nature of that meeting?"

"We were going to discuss a new ad campaign," he replied evenly. "She was supposed to come to the office here. Only she never showed up."

"Did she call or text to indicate she was having a problem with making the appointment?"

"No," he claimed. "I tried calling her, but she never picked up. I figured maybe she had her dates mixed up—it happens—or something else came up. I just planned to reschedule the meeting." He drew a breath. "I never imagined anything like that would have happened to her."

Annette felt he sounded credible enough, but still pressed ahead. "How long were you in the office that night?"

"Till around nine thirty or so," he answered. "I had some other business to attend to."

"Can anyone vouch for that?"

"Yeah." He looked at the woman on the phone. "My associate, Diane Fernandez, was here as well, the entire time."

Annette calculated the probable time of death, the location of where Lucy Beecham's body was found, miles away, and the likelihood that the real estate agency owner could have pulled this off successfully. Then there was the fact that his gray hair did not line up with the strands of dark hair believed to have come from the perpetrator in the last two murders.

When she left the office, Annette no longer considered Virgil Flynn a viable suspect worth pursuing.

HALF AN HOUR LATER, Annette met up with Hamilton at the Carol Creek Shopping Center where Ross Keach, whom Lucy had accused of sexually harassing her, was employed as a custodial worker. But had he graduated to something far more sinister?

Hamilton wanted to know the answer to that as much as Annette did, if not more. Especially after the forensic evidence had shown that Juliet's killer had also been the culprit in Lucy Beecham's murder and all but certainly was responsible for the ligature strangulation killings of JoBeth Sorenson and Yancy Machado. Now was the time to end this, if possible, by getting the perp off the streets once and for all.

In the mall, they spotted a tall and solidly built male who looked to be in his early thirties with dark locks in an angular fringe haircut and blue-gray eyes. Dressed in a maintenance uniform, he was pushing around a rolling trash cart, picking up litter along the way.

"You think that's him?" Annette whispered, as they approached.

"One way to find out," Hamilton told her.

Taking the lead, she got the attention of the custodial worker who seemed to be caught up in his own thoughts, saying to him, "Ross Keach?"

He shot her a cold stare. "Yeah. Who's asking?"

Annette flashed her identification. "Detective Lynley with the Dabs County Sheriff's Department," she answered. "State Trooper McCade. We'd like to—"

Before Annette could complete her sentence, Keach surprised them by pushing her hard enough into Hamilton that they both went tumbling down to the floor as Keach took off running. Hamilton's first concern, of course, was Annette, who seemed shaken up. "Are you okay?" he asked, while still beneath her, having taken the brunt of the fall.

"I'm good," she insisted, still clinging to him. "Did he hurt you?"

Under other circumstances, Hamilton would have welcomed this nearness to her. In this case, though, it went against the grain because it had been forced upon them by a serial killer suspect. He admitted, "Got the wind knocked out of me, but I was able to brace for the fall at the last instant. No major damage."

"I'm glad," Annette murmured.

He gently lifted her off him and both got to their feet in time to see the suspect running down the shopping center. "Let's go get him," Hamilton said, determined to nab Ross Keach, even if the man had gotten a nice head start.

"Right behind you," she shot back as they ran after the suspect.

They were in lockstep as Hamilton and Annette raced across the mall, dodging shoppers, while narrowing the gap between them and Keach. As they drew closer, the suspect began shoving people to the floor and flipping products on display in a desperate effort to slow them down.

Hamilton watched as Keach darted into a crowded department store, suspecting that his intention was to reach the door that led to a parking lot and then vanish. They couldn't allow him to do that. "We'd better split up," Hamilton told Annette, confident that the detective was more than capable of handling herself in this instance.

"I'm already ahead of you. I'll see if I can cut him off that way," she said, indicating another direction.

"And I'll try to get to the exit before he does."

They separated and went after Ross Keach, while Hamilton hoped no one else got hurt in the process. As he took long strides through aisles, past clothing racks, toys, and Christmas displays, Hamilton spotted the suspect, who had managed to create a real mess by tossing things at him and to the floor in his effort to escape. There was no indication that Keach was brandishing a firearm, which was a relief, since that could really turn this chase into a nightmare.

After Keach pushed through the exit to the outside and was about to break into a full stride in getting away, Annette tackled him from behind, seemingly coming out of nowhere and anticipating his moves. Caught completely off guard, Keach went down hard, with Annette on top of him. She quickly twisted one of his arms behind him and cuffed him, then did the same with the other.

When he caught up to them, Hamilton heard Annette reading Ross Keach his rights.

"Good job," Hamilton told her, impressed, as he roughly pulled the huffing and puffing suspect to his feet and made sure there were no further attempts at escape.

Annette bristled. "You do what you have to do."

Hamilton grinned. "And you do it well."

"Let's bring him in," she spat.

"Your car or mine?" Hamilton asked, half-jokingly.

Annette pursed her lips. "You pick."

He was more than happy to toss the suspect in the secure back seat of his patrol car. Then see what he had to say during interrogation as it related to the Christmas Lights Killer and the murder of Hamilton's niece.

IN THE INTERVIEW ROOM, Annette sat beside Will, across from Ross Keach, who was handcuffed and had remained stone-faced ever since being brought in for questioning in the murder of Lucy Beecham and presumably three other serial murders. Observing the interrogation through a one-way window was Hamilton, along with Sheriff Dillon Teixeira and Detective Charisma Robinson.

Annette was still a little sore from first being pushed onto Hamilton at the shopping center and then having to use leg muscles that didn't get as much of a workout during the winter-time. Tackling Keach actually felt pretty good after what he had put them through. His efforts to evade them had necessitated an arrest, with the initial charge of assaulting a member of law enforcement. She wondered how many more charges they could tack on.

After a moment or two of collecting her thoughts, Annette regarded the suspect sharply and said, "Let's start by talking about Lucy Bee-cham."

Keach furrowed his brow. "Who?"

Annette repeated the name and added, "The assistant general manager for McKinnon Marketing who got you fired after you sexually harassed her. Does that ring a bell?"

"Yeah, I remember that bitch," he sneered. "What about her?"

"Two nights ago, she was strangled to death," Will told him toughly. "You immediately became the number one suspect."

Keach's head snapped back. "I didn't kill anyone," he alleged. "I had nothing to do with her death."

Annette gave little credibility to his words of denial, which most murderers were quick to fall on like a sword. "If that's true, why did you run?"

He waited a beat, then responded shakily, "I

got into a fight with a neighbor who was making too much noise. I thought he'd pressed charges. When you told me you were cops, guess I just panicked."

Will glared at him dismissively. "You expect us to believe that?"

"Yeah, it's the truth," he maintained. "Neighbor's name is George Schneider. You can ask him."

"We intend to," Annette said tersely. "Right now, we'd like to ask where you were two nights ago, between eight and ten?" She believed it was more likely than not that Lucy would have been killed shortly after she went missing than later.

Keach lifted his cuffed hands and rubbed his jaw. "I went for a drink after work that day," he claimed.

"Where?" she demanded.

"The Penn Street Bar. I was there till at least midnight."

"I assume others can verify this?"

"Yeah, sure," he said. "The bartender, for one. He tried to cut me off, but I kept the drinks coming."

Annette glanced at the one-way mirror, wondering what the sheriff and Hamilton were thinking, and back to the suspect. "Would you be willing to give us a DNA sample?"

Keach wavered. "Why should I?"

"Because it would go a long way in eliminating you as a suspect in as many as four murders of women in town," she told him bluntly. "Otherwise, you'll be spending the night in jail for assaulting two officers of the law, pending verification of your alibi and statements. That's assuming we can't find new evidence linking you to Lucy Beecham's murder before then."

"I'll give you my DNA." Keach jutted his chin. "If that doesn't do the trick, I want a lawyer," he said for the first time.

Annette looked at Will. By his expression, she could tell that, like her, he didn't believe that Ross Keach was their man in Lucy's death. Or the Christmas Lights Killer.

HE HADN'T MEANT for things to end that way for the latest victim. Actually, he had. Just not the manner in which it all played out. He'd been so excited in getting the jump on her that, after forcing her into the back seat of his car, he had failed to use the master lock to keep her from escaping. This had nearly cost him when he'd been forced to stop abruptly to avoid hitting a deer. She'd taken full advantage of this by getting out and making a run for it.

Fortunately for him, she hadn't gotten very far. Before she could break into a full jaunt in the wooded area, he had managed to trip her, but had himself fallen in the process. But he'd recovered more quickly than her and gotten back on his feet. While she'd made a valiant attempt to crawl away, he would have none of it. Not when her survival would go completely against his own agenda in taking her life.

With the Christmas lights in hand, he'd pounced on her like a leopard and, with lightning speed, wrapped the string around her pretty little neck, twisting, turning, and tightening as she struggled to breathe, till any fight she had left in her faded like fog. Admittedly, the experience had given him a new thrill and reason to celebrate yet another successful kill.

As for those pursuing him, he could only laugh at their ineptness. Going off course in their attempts to apprehend him only worked in his favor. He was enjoying this way too much to let them stand in his way. Or interfere with his plans. No, there needed to be others to die by the power vested in him with help from the Christmas string lights. Carol Creek might never be the same again. Not his problem. This was simply the way it had to be.

He drove nowhere in particular, but everywhere the car could take him. It wasn't exactly a joy ride, but would be when the time was right to strike again. In the meantime, he sat back, took in the sights of Christmastime and found himself singing along with the Christmas classic tune that played in his head.

Chapter Fourteen

After Ross Keach's DNA failed to match that taken from the strands of hair connected to two murders and his alibi held up, he was released. Though Annette was beyond frustrated, she was more concerned with apprehending the real serial killer than putting away an innocent man. She had no doubt that Hamilton was of the same mind, as was Sheriff Teixeira. They were doing the right thing by investigating all leads and, when going nowhere, moving on to other possible evidence and suspects that could crack the case.

What Annette didn't want to do at this point was allow the unsub to ruin her Christmas altogether. That would be giving one person way too much power that was totally undeserving. As such, she decided to put up a small Christmas tree as a prelude to the larger one she could expect for the family gathering. She invited Hamilton to decorate it with her and then make dinner for him, believing they could both use some time together after another long day.

Hamilton was quick to accept the invite and they picked out a tabletop miniature pine Christmas tree that came with ornaments and a small treetop star. Setting it on the vintage country coffee table, they decorated while listening to some Nat King Cole holiday music and sipping wine.

"So, what do you think?" Annette asked when they were done.

Hamilton smiled. "I think it looks great and it's a good enhancement for your place at this time of year."

"You're right. Maybe next year, I'll get a great big one that can really get me into the spirit of Christmas."

"Maybe next year, we'll be able to take on that task together," he suggested boldly.

She eyed him with a tingle inside at the possibilities. "Oh, you think so, huh?"

"Hey, Christmas is all about believing in remarkable things, right?"

You are so right, Annette thought dreamily. "Of course." She wondered if, in a year, things really would have progressed to the point of them living under the same roof. And exactly which roof would that be?

"So, what do you say we make that meal together?" Hamilton suggested, tasting the wine. "I'm starving!"

She raised a brow. "Are you sure you wouldn't prefer to just sit back and relax and leave the cooking up to me this time?"

He made a playful face. "Now, what fun would that be?"

She laughed. "Never really considered cooking fun, per se. But maybe with you, it could be."

"Only one way to put that to the test," he challenged her.

Taking him up on that, Annette happily gave way to his zest for doing this together and welcomed him into her kitchen as an equal. They managed to take what she had in the refrigerator and made macaroni and cheese, tomato basil soup, and barbecue meatballs. After wining and dining, even feeding each other, they went to bed and made love. Annette gave as much as she took, thrilling in the closeness of their bodies and sense of knowing what the other needed and when to act upon those impulses. When their climaxes came, both seized the long moment to relish in complete unison.

Afterward, Hamilton hummed, "I could get used to this."

"Oh, really?" Annette looked at him. "Just here and at your cabin? When do we get to take this show to your house in Fort Wayne?" She hoped she wasn't being too pushy, but needed to know just how strongly committed he was to giving this a go.

"Anytime you like." He kissed her shoulder. "You're always welcome at my house. I'd love for you to see it."

Her lashes fluttered. "You sure about that?"

"Positive. I would've invited you over sooner, but between the distance from Carol Creek and an ongoing investigation, I thought you might turn me down."

"I wouldn't have," she told him, though his rationale made sense.

"Then consider this an invitation to take our show to my humble abode tonight or whenever."

Annette smiled, more than satisfied that this truly did seem to be headed toward something serious. "Invitation accepted," she told him gleefully.

Hamilton grinned back at her and they cuddled, before exhaustion overtook them and they fell asleep.

In the morning, Annette allowed Hamilton to get some extra shut-eye while she dressed and made breakfast, feeling very much like it was a normal thing these days to have a man in her bed. He had made it seem that way. Definitely gave them something to build upon. She hoped he liked waffles with real maple syrup and bacon.

When her cell phone buzzed, Annette lifted it from the soapstone countertop and saw that the caller was her nonbiological first cousin, Gavin Lynley. She accepted the video chat request. He appeared and she took in his handsome rectangular face. Biracial and two years her senior, Gavin was gray-eyed and had short, jet-black hair in a lineup cut and a five-o'clock shadow beard.

"Hey, stranger," she said, smiling.

"Hey, Detective," he tossed back at her. "What's up?"

"You tell me." Annette narrowed her eyes teasingly. "Can we expect you at the family Christmas gathering or not?"

"Yeah," he promised. "Wouldn't miss it."

"Well, good." She grinned. "Lots to catch up on."

"Looking forward to it." Gavin angled his face slightly. "So, what's the latest on the serial killer investigation I've been hearing about?"

"I'll need to get back to you on that," Annette told him, realizing it would take more time than she had right now. Not to mention, she would rather there was more definitive info to share later. "And then you can also fill me in on the latest from a special agent."

"Deal," he said understandingly. "Catch you soon."

They said their goodbyes and she disconnected, just as Hamilton walked into the kitchen, fully dressed. "Good morning," she told him with a smile.

"Morning, beautiful." He walked up to her and gave her a kiss. "Who was on the phone?" he asked curiously.

"My cousin Gavin. The one I told you worked in corrections."

"Ah." Hamilton nodded. "So, guess I'll have to pass muster with your large family when all is said and done, huh?"

Annette chuckled. "I don't know about all that," she half joked. "But I'm sure they'll like you and vice versa."

"Good." He grabbed a slice of bacon and bit into it. "I think you've already won over Maureen."

She lifted a brow. "Is that so?"

"Don't seem so surprised." He laughed. "My sister's always had good instincts, for the most part. In this case, she sees you as a really good catch. And I agree."

Annette blushed. "That works both ways. I see the same in you and I'm glad Maureen can appreciate what I bring to the table," she added gratefully.

"Speaking of which, feel free to bring those waffles to the table whenever you're ready," he said jovially.

"Coming right up." She lifted a steaming waffle and put it on a plate. "You can get your own coffee."

He grinned. "Will do."

HAMILTON FELT THAT things were starting to heat up with Annette. Spending the night at her house was certainly a step up the ladder. Now she wanted to see where he lived and he was more than happy to oblige. If things continued to move in the right direction, they might eventually need to decide where to live together and under what circumstances. He felt this was the right time in his life to think in those terms with this person. And even if he had to fight his way through Annette's siblings and other relatives to win her heart, Hamilton was more than ready to duke it out and win.

But right now, both he and Annette were on the case in trying to put this serial killer investigation to rest. With another victim added to the Christmas Lights Killer's list, it was obvious to Hamilton that they were dealing with a monster of the worst kind, one who was seemingly itching to continue targeting women in

Carol Creek throughout the holiday season and likely into the new year.

Hamilton was parked along the side of the road, looking for violators of the state's Move Over Slow Down Law, designed to protect emergency and highway workers from harm. He hoped drivers behaved themselves this morning. His thoughts were interrupted by a call from another ISP member on the Christmas Lights Killer task force, Kendre Fitzgerald, who had been studying surveillance videos at retailers across the state in search of buyers of Christmas string lights in the past few months.

"McCade," he said.

"Hey, I found something that you may want to see."

"Okay."

"It's security camera footage from a store in Indianapolis taken in mid-November," she said. "I'm sending it to you now."

Hamilton opened his tablet and received the video footage. It showed a slender, dark-haired man who looked to be in his early thirties, purchasing two or three sets of indoor Christmas string lights. And using cash to pay for it. Nothing suspicious in that, per se. But something about the man rubbed Hamilton the wrong way.

"What do you think?" Kendre asked eagerly.

"I'm thinking that the customer is rather

suspicious," he responded honestly. Hamilton zoomed in on the man's face. Though this made the face grainier, there was an air of familiarity about it that he couldn't miss. If this was their unsub, the timeline for purchasing the indoor string lights would fit. This was before the serial killings began. And buying the lights outside of Carol Creek, or Fort Wayne for that matter, would make sense, too. This would make it harder to connect the dots in identifying the perp. "Find out everything you can about this buyer," Hamilton told her. "And double-check other stores between Indianapolis and Fort Wayne to see if the same customer shows up on surveillance video purchasing Christmas string lights. If so, maybe he used a credit card for some buys."

"I'll get right on it," Kendre told him.

"Thanks, and good work," Hamilton commended her before disconnecting. He took a second look at the video footage and again wondered if he could have seen the customer before somewhere. And if this could actually be their serial killer.

ANNETTE AND WILL went to an address on Cetona Way, whose occupant, a woman named Vera Cardwell, was listed as the registered owner of a black Ford Bronco Sport Big Bend with Goodyear Wrangler Fortitude HT tires. They walked up the path toward the colonial-style home, when Annette noted the white Lincoln Nautilus parked in the driveway. It made her wonder if the Ford Bronco they had come in search of could have been sold or replaced.

She rang the bell and the door opened a crack. A slender, elderly woman, wearing square glasses over blue eyes, peeked out and said cautiously, "May I help you?"

Annette held her badge up to where she could see it. "Detective Lynley, and this is Detective Hossack of the Sheriff's Department. Are you Vera Cardwell?"

"Yes."

"We need to ask you some questions regarding the Ford Bronco Sport Big Bend registered to you."

Vera considered this for a moment or two before opening the door and inviting them inside. Annette took a quick glance around the gray-carpeted living room. It was full of contemporary furnishings and decorated for the holidays, including a northern white cedar Christmas tree. She faced the homeowner, who had an ash-blond layered bob, and was leaning on an aluminum walking cane.

Vera seemed ill at ease. "What about my Bronco?"

"Do you still have it?" Annette inquired.

"Yes, though I rarely use it anymore. Mind telling me what's going on here?"

Will stepped forward. "We're investigating some recent homicides," he spoke candidly. "We have reason to believe that the person responsible was driving a vehicle with the type of Goodyear tires you have. All we're doing here is going down the line of anyone owning such a vehicle for the process of elimination. No big deal," he tried to say as though true.

Annette jumped in again. "You said you rarely drive your Ford Bronco." She assumed this was due to Vera driving the Lincoln instead. "Does anyone else drive it?"

"Only my grandson, on occasion," she replied unevenly.

"Does your grandson live with you?"

"No. I've lived alone since my husband, Henry, died. Mack has his own apartment. Sometimes he'll drive the Bronco when his own car is giving him problems. Or when he's running an errand for me."

"His name is Mack?" Will asked.

"Yes. Mack Cardwell."

"How old is Mack?" Annette asked in a friendly voice.

"Thirty-two," Vera replied.

Annette pondered that for a moment and asked, "Where is the car now?"

"In the garage. It's too cold to keep it out during the winter months."

Will raised a brow. "Mind if we have a look?"

Vera nodded. "The garage is right through that door," she said, pointing to a door in a hallway off the kitchen. "I don't think you'll find what you're looking for, though. Mack's a good boy and wouldn't hurt anyone."

That's what they all say, Annette thought. Until proven otherwise. "Hope you're right about that," she told her sincerely.

Annette and Will stepped into the garage, turning on the light. A vehicle was hidden beneath a black waterproof car cover. Will put on nitrile gloves and lifted the cover, revealing the Ford Bronco Sport Big Bend. "Wonder why he felt the need to cover it in a garage?"

"Hmm…" Annette asked herself the same question, even while knowing there was nothing suspicious about someone wanting to protect a car and keep the dust off even indoors. There was no outer sign of damage to the vehicle. She studied the tires. Though they displayed the typical dirt and grime from driving, there was nothing that drew red flags.

Will, who had opened the passenger-side door, said, "Take a look at this."

Annette looked inside and saw a tiny spot on the front seat that looked like it could be blood. Had a passenger bled? Under what circumstances? "Could be blood," she said what they both were thinking. But they had no grounds at present to have it tested. Other than that, the inside front and back of the car looked pristine, as though it had been cleaned purposely. So, what was the story on the grandson anyway? Should he be considered a suspect? Or were they getting ahead of themselves? "Put the cover back on the vehicle," she told Will. "It'll keep it protected in case we need to come back later for forensic testing."

They went back inside, where Vera was now sitting tensely on a rocker recliner. Annette asked her, "When was the last time your grandson drove the Bronco?"

"Two or three days ago, I think." Vera squirmed. "Mack's never been in any trouble," she insisted. "Since his girlfriend left him last year, all he's wanted to do was put the past behind him and make a better life for himself with someone else."

Annette knew all about sour relationships and moving on, having done so with Hamilton, and she couldn't be more excited about the prospects for where this could go. But not all people dealt with broken relationships the same way.

Could Mack Cardwell have been on some sort of warped, murderous revenge crusade? "We're going to need to speak with your grandson," she told Vera. "Once we've done so, we'll be able to cross your vehicle off the list." Annette hoped that would be enough to alleviate the concerns of the grandmother. At least till they could officially eliminate Cardwell as a suspect.

Twenty minutes later, Annette and Will drove to an apartment complex called Crow's Village on Wailby Crest Lane in the adjacent town of Laraville in Dabs County. They went up to the second-story unit where Mack Cardwell lived.

"Sheriff's Department," Will yelled, knocking on the door.

After a couple of more knocks and hearing no sounds coming from within, Annette surmised, "I don't think he's here."

Will frowned. "Too bad. I'd love to hear what Cardwell has to say. Or not."

"Me, too." She took out a pen and her detective's card and wrote a note to the suspect on the back that he needed to get in touch with her as soon as possible. She stuck the card inside the door and thought, *If you have nothing to hide, I'll hear from you shortly.* "Let's go," she told Will.

He nodded and knocked one more time on

Cardwell's door for effect, and muttered, "I have a feeling we may need to come back here."

As she mulled that over, Annette's cell phone rang. She removed it from the pocket of her leather jacket and answered, "Lynley."

It was Detective Charisma Robinson on the other end. "We've had another woman attacked," she said shakily.

"Oh no…" Annette eyed Will, with the worst-case scenario playing on her mind. "Is she—?"

"The victim's still alive," Charisma responded. "She's been taken to Carol Creek General."

"We're on our way." Annette disconnected and faced Will. "It looks like he has struck again." Will muttered an expletive under his breath. "But the victim has survived, though I have no idea what kind of shape she's in."

Still, it gave Annette a glimmer of hope that the woman would pull through and be able to assist them. She phoned Hamilton to update him on the latest news.

Chapter Fifteen

When he got word that another woman had been targeted and had apparently lived to talk about it, Hamilton headed straight for the hospital. The fact that the serial killer seemed to be picking up the pace was troubling, to say the least. He was getting desperate to go after anyone who crossed his path, making him all the more dangerous.

At Carol Creek General on Femmore Avenue, Hamilton raced inside and spotted Annette, Will and Charisma converged in the lobby. Walking up to them, Hamilton said, "Any word on the victim?"

"She's being treated by a doctor, but is expected to pull through with little more than a mild concussion and a few bumps and bruises," Annette said, relief crossing her face. "The mental trauma of going through something like that is another matter altogether."

Hamilton concurred. "What do we know about her?"

"The victim's name is Gemma Jeong," Charisma said. "She's a twenty-nine-year-old graphic artist, married to an estate planning attorney named Remy Jeong, and the mother of two children."

"How did she manage to escape the killer?" Will asked.

"Good question. Haven't had the chance to ask her yet."

"We should know soon enough." Annette sighed. "I think we can all agree that surviving a serial killer, if in fact that's what this was, is a miracle in and of itself."

Hamilton nodded and couldn't help but think about Juliet, who hadn't been able to wrest herself from harm's way. He would give anything to have had that happen, but it wasn't meant to be. But she could rest in peace more comfortably once her killer was put away for good. "I have other news," he told them. "Some surveillance video has been accessed by an ISP investigator that shows a suspect purchasing Christmas string lights at an Indianapolis store."

Annette's eyes widened. "You think he could be the guy?"

"Yes, it's possible, given that he was purchasing more than one set and the date of purchase was just before the murders began." Hamilton shifted his feet. "More than that, I think I recognize the image of the buyer as someone I stopped recently for having a misplaced license plate in his car window."

"We have a possible lead, too," Annette informed him. "Will and I went to talk to the owner of a Ford Bronco Sport Big Bend with Goodyear Wrangler Fortitude HT tires. She said that it's driven mostly by her thirty-two-year-old grandson, including apparently driving the vehicle the night Lucy Beecham was murdered."

Will gritted his teeth. "We dropped by his apartment, but he wasn't there."

"What's his name?" Hamilton asked.

Annette answered, "Mack Cardwell."

"He's the same person—Mack Anthony Cardwell—I stopped recently on the road in Fort Wayne," Hamilton told them. "I'm almost certain he's the one on the video footage at the Indianapolis store."

"What kind of car was he driving when you pulled him over?" Will asked.

Hamilton furrowed his brow. "Actually, it was a Dodge Challenger," he almost hated to say.

Annette wrinkled her nose. "So, not the Ford Bronco?"

"Afraid not." He considered this discrepancy. "Doesn't mean that Cardwell couldn't have still switched from one vehicle to another to suit his purposes or as a cover."

"Anything's possible at this point," Charisma muttered.

"Guess we need to see what Gemma Jeong has to say and if she can identify her assailant," Annette said.

"Yeah." Hamilton prepared himself for disappointment, but his gut instincts told him that there may be something to the belief that Mack Anthony Cardwell was up to no good and could well be the devious serial killer.

WHEN THEY WERE able to speak directly with Gemma Jeong, the doctor only allowed two people in the room at a time, apart from Gemma's husband, Remy. As lead investigator, Annette went in, with Hamilton joining her.

Gemma, a slender, attractive Asian woman, was half sitting up in the bed. She had shoulder-length, wavy brown hair and dark brown eyes. Considering her ordeal, Annette thought that the graphic artist looked pretty good physically. Remy, who was tall, lean, and looked to be thirtysomething, had black hair in a spiky cut. He was holding her hand.

Though Annette wished she didn't have to cut in on the couple's loving moment, now was the time to hear what she could tell them, when the victim's mind was freshest. "Mrs. Jeong, I'm Detective Lynley with the sheriff's office," she said, showing her badge. "This is State Trooper McCade. We'd like to ask you a few questions about what happened."

Remy frowned. "Can't this wait?"

"We wish it could, but someone apparently tried to kill your wife," Hamilton responded brusquely. "No guarantee he won't try again as long as he remains on the loose."

"I'll talk to them," Gemma said. "This needs to be done" she told her husband. "If there's anything I can do to get that creep off the streets, I want to do it."

Remy relented. "Try to keep it brief."

"We will." Annette glanced at Hamilton and turned back to the victim. "Can you tell us what happened?"

Gemma sucked in a deep breath and said, "At just after eleven, I left my shop on Owen Point Drive to go to lunch. I was about to get into my car, when seemingly out of nowhere, this man is standing there. He asked me for directions and as I was trying to give them, he was suddenly holding some Christmas string lights. He told me he was going to strangle me with them and that I shouldn't fight it."

"But you did?" Hamilton prompted her.

"Yes, my first instincts were to scratch his

face. I tried, but only managed to scrape my fingers across his neck. It was enough to draw blood." She sighed. "He called me a bitch and seemed enraged, hitting me and shoving me to the ground. He was about to put the string lights around my neck, but when a security guard came into the lot and yelled at the man to stop, he took off and got away. I called 911 and was taken to the hospital."

Annette locked eyes with Hamilton in this remarkable story of survival against the odds. "We need to get the statement of the security guard," she told her.

Gemma nodded. "His name is Nestor Bedelia. He gave me his cell phone number and is waiting to hear from you." Her eyes watered. "He saved my life."

As Hamilton got Bedelia's number, Annette asked Gemma, "Do you happen to know if the attacker got into a vehicle after running off?"

"I couldn't say. I was too shaken up to notice."

Annette knew that the unsub couldn't have been driving the Ford Bronco Sport Big Bend that seemed to be tied to at least two of the earlier attacks, given that the car was still inside Vera Cardwell's garage when the attack occurred. Meaning if her grandson was the culprit here, he would have either been on foot or was driving another vehicle for his getaway car. "Had you ever seen your attacker before?"

Gemma rubbed her hand and Annette could see what appeared to be dried blood beneath two of her long fingernails, likely from scratching the unsub. "Not that I can recall." Gemma paused. "It's possible, though, since we get people in and out of the shop all the time. Or it could have been elsewhere."

"Can you describe him?" Hamilton asked.

"Yes. He was tall—maybe six feet—and somewhat slight in build." Gemma mused for a moment. "His hair was dark and in a messy style, while short on the sides."

Annette gazed at her. "Any hair on his face?"

"Yes, he had a short beard."

Annette looked at Hamilton and this seemed to register with him. "Do you happen to remember the type of clothing he was wearing?"

"Didn't really focus on that," Gemma admitted. "But I think he had on a dark jacket, jeans, and maybe tennis shoes."

"If it's all right with you," Annette told her, "we'd like to get a sketch artist in here to help you flush out a few more details on your attacker that can help us track him down."

She nodded in agreement. "I'll try my best."

"And we'd also like to collect a sample of the DNA beneath your nails that I assume came from the attacker," Annette said. "That could be important in making the case against him."

"Yeah, sure." Gemma winced, as though in sudden discomfort.

Remy narrowed his eyes and said, "That's enough for now."

"Okay." Annette didn't dare press any further. They had what was needed for the time being in furthering the investigation. "Thanks for giving us your statement," she told Gemma. "We'll try to get the man who attacked you."

Gemma wiped away tears. "Hope so."

Once they were out of the room, Annette regarded Hamilton and asked, "What do you think?"

"Her description seems to fit Mack Cardwell's appearance. We'll need to see what the sketch artist can produce."

"And see if the DNA the assailant left is a match for the DNA collected from the strands of hair from two of the other murders," she said thoughtfully.

"I think we need to pay Cardwell another visit," Will said. "See if he'll talk and provide a DNA sample voluntarily."

Charisma rolled her eyes. "Good luck with that. If Cardwell is guilty, he's not likely to be very cooperative."

Annette was inclined to agree. They would

need to be prepared to get a search warrant to collect any potential evidence needed against Cardwell. Assuming he remained a viable suspect after the sketch artist's drawing and the forensic evidence from Gemma Jeong was analyzed. Otherwise, the onus would be on them to track down the culprit elsewhere.

They learned that the doctor intended to keep Gemma in the hospital overnight as a precaution. With her assailant still at large, Annette was taking no chances with her safety even at the hospital, given the perp's hunger for killing and winning. "I want a deputy stationed outside this room," she told everyone, "and even at Gemma's house, as long as the suspect is on the loose. As the only living witness who can identify him, apart from possibly the security guard, the perp may stop at nothing to make certain that doesn't happen."

"I'll get the deputy here and notify the staff as well to be on the lookout for anyone suspicious," Will assured her.

"And I'll make sure that forensics gets the unsub's DNA," Charisma said, running a hand through her hair. "I'm pretty sure that we're looking at the same DNA profile in the database. We just need to see if we can line it up with the latest suspect."

It was something very much on Annette's

mind, too. If they could tie this to Mack Cardwell, then there would be nowhere he could hide before they brought him in and held him accountable as a serial killer.

LATER, HAMILTON SAT in Annette's office as they reviewed the case and latest turn of events. Both were gratified that whoever attacked Gemma Jeong had failed to kill her and would never be given the chance to do so again. The question remained in Hamilton's mind, who was the unsub and presumed serial killer? He had strong suspicions about the man's identity, but needed solid evidence to back this up.

When Jenn Eugenio walked into the office, Hamilton met the brown eyes of the thirtysomething forensic artist, who was petite and had black hair with brown highlights in a short and straight style. She was carrying her drawing tablet. Offering him and Annette a smile, Jenn said, "Hey, guys."

"What do you have for us?" Hamilton asked anxiously.

"Well, I'm happy to say that the victim did a pretty good job of describing the man who attacked her, with my prodding for as many details as she could remember. Here's what we came up with."

Annette, who had been sitting at her desk,

stood and walked around it so she and Hamilton could view the image at the same time. "What do you think?" she asked him curiously.

He studied the digital image that bore some resemblance to the man he knew as Mack Anthony Cardwell. "It could be Cardwell," he responded, "or someone who fits his general features, as I recall."

"That's enough justification to go on that assumption," Annette said, "when coupled with the video footage you've seen of someone fitting that description and the fact that we're still trying to make contact with Cardwell to question him about the Ford Bronco he's been driving intermittently." She eyed Jenn. "We need to get this out to all the law enforcement in the state, as well as local media. Whether the unsub is Cardwell or someone else, his image needs to be put forth as a person of interest who has to be considered armed and dangerous. Though his weapon of choice has been Christmas string lights, we have to assume he may also have a firearm in his possession."

"I'll get the ball rolling," Jenn promised. "And send you both copies of the sketch as well."

"Good work," Hamilton told her, which she acknowledged before leaving the office.

Annette's cell phone rang with a call from Kelly Okamoto, from the ISP Fort Wayne Regional Laboratory. She had put a rush on analyzing the DNA removed from underneath Gemma Jeong's nails. Annette put Kelly on speakerphone and said, "You're on speaker and I'm with Trooper Hamilton McCade. What did you find out?"

Without prelude, Kelly responded, "The analysis of the genetic material found under the victim's fingernails showed a DNA match with the forensic unknown profile connected to the hair strands collected from Juliet McCade and Lucy Beecham. Or, in other words, all three DNA samples belong to the same unsub."

In Hamilton's way of thinking, this lent itself even more strongly to the notion that Mack Anthony Cardwell was the likely perp, when tying it to the circumstantial evidence pointing in his direction. But the latest info still fell short of proving that conclusively, with nothing in CODIS to support this as Cardwell's DNA.

As though reading his mind, Kelly said flatly, "If you want to attach the DNA findings to a suspect in particular, you need to bring me his actual DNA for comparison and you'll have your answer."

"We hear you," Hamilton told her, before the conversation ended.

Afterward, Annette put her hand on his

shoulder and said firmly, "We need to bring Mack Cardwell in for questioning."

"I agree," he stated, resisting the desire to touch her. "First, we have to find him."

"Beyond that, I think we have more than enough to get a judge to sign off on a search warrant at his apartment." She folded her arms. "If we can't get Cardwell to voluntarily hand over his DNA, we'll have to legally obtain it, and gather any other evidence that may pertain to our investigation."

"I'm with you." Hamilton got to his feet. He wanted to take her into his arms at that moment. But they were in duty mode and he needed to act accordingly, hard as that was whenever he was in her presence. "Let's go find that judge."

Chapter Sixteen

After Judge Suzanne Manaois-Seatriz approved the search warrant, Annette, Will and Hamilton went to the apartment of Mack Anthony Cardwell, accompanied by other armed law enforcement and forensic investigators. With no sign of Cardwell's black Dodge Challenger SRT Hellcat Redeye, the assumption was that he was not home, perhaps deliberately avoiding them. They knocked on the door anyhow, while Annette identified herself and others. When there was no reply, the order was given to use a Halligan bar to force the door open.

Inside, Annette held her Glock 43 9mm pistol in front of her as she stood on the laminate flooring and surveyed the two-bedroom, traditionally furnished unit. It was cluttered and reeked of the pungent scent of marijuana. On a coffee table was drug paraphernalia and what looked to be crystal methamphetamine along with a number of fentanyl pills. Strewn across a rust-colored armchair was a set of Christmas string lights resembling those used to strangle four women and also fitting the description of the lights that had been used in the attempt to strangle Gemma Jeong. Were those the very same string lights used in the crimes?

Wonder how Cardwell would care to explain himself, with the potentially incriminating Christmas string lights in his home, Annette mused with skepticism. The man was also facing possible charges for felony drug possession.

"Clear!" Will yelled from one of the rooms after going through the apartment.

Annette lowered her weapon and placed it back in the holster as Hamilton came up behind her and said, "Looks like Cardwell may have been dealing drugs, at the very least."

"Or it's just the tip of the iceberg in his criminal behavior," she countered, and directed Hamilton's attention to the chair. "Who has Christmas string lights hanging around when the apartment is otherwise devoid of any holiday decorations? Unless Cardwell has them with another devious purpose in mind."

"I was thinking the same thing," Hamilton said. "And we both know what that is."

Annette nodded. "Could he have anticipated us showing up here and made sure he was nowhere to be found?"

"He may or may not be on to us, but we're definitely on to him." Hamilton put away his SIG Sauer P227 pistol.

"Something tells me Cardwell's probably already figured that out," she hated to say, "whether tipped off intentionally or inadvertently by his grandmother, Vera Cardwell. Or his own instincts in believing he's smarter than us."

"Not even close." Hamilton's brows lowered. "He's simply been luckier than us. Till now, that is. If Cardwell's who we believe him to be, his DNA will corroborate this and we'll have him dead to rights as the Christmas Lights Killer."

"That would certainly be the best gift any of us could have," Annette contended. Short of Hamilton giving her the gift of his love and wanting them to become official as a couple. Or was that asking too much of him? Or herself?

He flashed her a look. "You've got that right."

Loretta Covington approached them, coming out of the bathroom. "I have what we need to get the suspect's DNA," the forensic analyst said. Wearing latex gloves, she was holding a plastic evidence bag. "A toothbrush, razor and some hair samples he left in a filthy sink."

"Good." Annette smiled at her. "If Mack Cardwell has something to hide, this would likely blow that out of the water."

"That's what I'm hoping for." Loretta nodded.

"Let's get it to the crime lab ASAP," Hamilton said with urgency. "We need to know, like yesterday, if Cardwell's DNA matches the blood Gemma Jeong got from her attacker when she scratched him."

Not to mention, the hair removed from Juliet's mouth, Annette told herself, reading Hamilton's mind. As well as a second hair linked to the same unsub. The clock was ticking and they all felt the pressure to wrap up this case with an arrest that could stand up.

HAMILTON INVITED ANNETTE over to his house while they waited for word on the DNA results. Neither was making any predictions, even if both were optimistic that Cardwell's DNA profile would be a match with the unsub's and prove to be the ammunition they needed to bring him in.

In the interim, Hamilton was happy to show Annette that she was more than welcome to spend as much time at his place as she wanted. Hell, if he had his way, she could just move right in with him. Or would he need to go even further in demonstrating how much she meant to him? Did she feel the same level of commitment?

"I love your house," she commented, favoring him with a generous smile.

"Glad you like it," he said sincerely.

"Hope to spend more time here."

"I hope so, too."

She moved up to him. "You sure I wouldn't be cramping your style as a single man?"

"Positive." He grinned, but became serious again. "Besides, who says I'm a single man? On the contrary, I'm pretty much spoken for these days."

"Is that so?" Annette lifted her face toward his tantalizingly. "So, who's the lucky lady?"

Hamilton held her chin. "I think you know the answer to that." But in case she didn't, he gave her a nice kiss, so as to leave no doubt. "It could only be you."

She licked her lips and giggled. "Just checking."

"No problem," he said, keeping his arousal in check.

Their banter was put on hold when Annette's cell phone rang. It was Kelly Okamoto, who asked that they come to the crime lab. "Be right there," she told her.

"This better be good," Hamilton muttered, knowing this was make-or-break point in the investigation.

Annette nodded. "We'll know soon enough."

The short drive brought them to the lab's Forensic Biology Section, where Kelly was waiting. Impatiently, Hamilton asked her, "Well…?"

After a momentary deadpan look, the forensic scientist broke into a smile and responded, "It's a match! Mack Anthony Cardwell's DNA is an exact match for the other three DNA samples analyzed."

"I knew it!" Annette exclaimed gleefully.

"I strongly suspected as much," Hamilton agreed. "Cardwell is the Christmas Lights Killer."

"His reign of terror is about to end," Annette declared.

"Glad the lab was able to connect the forensic dots," Kelly told them.

"Me, too." Hamilton grinned. "Now we just need to finish this, once and for all."

"Right," Annette concurred, "before Cardwell can turn his deadly attention to someone else."

A BOLO was issued for Mack Anthony Cardwell, and the serial killer suspect's black Dodge Challenger SRT Hellcat Redeye, as well as a warrant to impound his grandmother's black Ford Bronco Sport Big Bend for to examine for forensic evidence that it was used to commit criminal activity pertaining to the investigation. Cardwell was considered armed and definitely dangerous. Annette certainly believed this to be the case and wouldn't put anything past the killer at this point. He obviously thought this could go on forever, no matter how many dead bodies he left in his wake. Well, his days of freedom to hunt and kill as he pleased were over.

Annette felt confident that the suspect would be picked up at anytime now. While awaiting word, she headed home from the sheriff's office, having already made plans to spend the night at Hamilton's house. They intended to make dinner together again. Perhaps beef lasagna and a garden salad. Only this time, in his kitchen, where he got to call the shots. Well, maybe they would have to negotiate on that. In her mind, just being with the man was more than enough to give and take a little. That was how it was supposed to be with couples who were in love.

Wait, did I just say I'm in love? Annette asked herself. Or, better yet, that it went both ways? She flushed at the notion and was hopeful at the same time that this was real between them. And that when this serial killer business was behind them, they could work more on each other and give what they had a real go.

That made her think about Christmas and her family reunion. Should she invite Hamilton? Or would that be inappropriate and insensitive due to his recent loss? But Maureen had taken her own holiday away from Carol Creek, as part of moving on with her life. Shouldn't Hamilton be entitled to do the same thing? *I'd love to introduce him to my siblings and cousin*, Annette thought. It was a big step, but worth it for someone she had really fallen for and seemed to be reciprocating her feelings in full measure.

Annette pulled into her driveway. She grabbed her shoulder tote containing some information pertaining to the investigation and headed inside the house. After turning on the lights, she set the tote on a table, pulled off her ankle booties and headed into the kitchen. There, she removed her firearm, laying it on the countertop for now. She would put it back in its holster to take with her to Hamilton's place, just to be on the safe side, after changing clothes.

Taking a bottle of red wine out of the refrigerator, Annette poured herself half a glass and went upstairs, where she took out her cell phone and gave her brother Russell a call. She owed him one, as they had limited themselves to texting of late, with each caught up in their own worlds. "Hey," she said.

"Annette." She could hear his voice perk up. "You better not be calling to say there's a last-minute change of plans for Christmas?"

She laughed. "Not in the way you think."

"Enlighten me."

Now was as good a time as any to mention she was seeing someone, Annette told herself, taking a sip of the wine. "I'm thinking about bringing someone to the family gathering."

"Hmm..." Russell hummed. "It wouldn't happen to be the state trooper Madison said you had the hots for, would it?"

I'm going to kill her, Annette thought playfully, while admiring her sister for interpreting correctly something that she had wisely picked up on. "I was supposed to spread the word when I was ready to," she complained nonetheless.

"Hey, don't blame me for Madison's inability to keep from reading the tea leaves and relating this in her own humorous way."

Annette couldn't help but chuckle at this, knowing her sister was well-intentioned. "Guess the cat's out of the bag."

"Guess it is. Or should I say, he is." Russell laughed. "In any event, I look forward to meeting him and introducing him to Rosamund."

"I want that, too," Annette admitted. But first Hamilton had to agree to it. She heard a faint sound downstairs, but couldn't figure out what it was. Or where it was coming from. A gust of wintry wind perhaps? Could she have forgotten to lock the door? It was probably nothing to concern herself with, but she should check it out anyway. "Let me call you back," she cut through Russell's easygoing chatter.

"Sure." He paused. "Everything okay?"

"Yeah, everything's fine." She saw no reason to worry him unnecessarily. Or herself, for that matter. After disconnecting, Annette headed down the stairs. Feeling tense for some reason, she went toward the front door and saw that it was locked. It hadn't slipped her mind after all. She let down her guard, but then heard another sound. It seemed to be coming from the kitchen area.

Annette stepped into the kitchen and, startled, dropped the glass of wine to the floor when she saw a man standing there. It took only an instant to realize it was the man they had fingered as the Christmas Lights Killer.

Mack Anthony Cardwell.

HAMILTON WAS DRIVING when he received word that Mack Cardwell's Dodge Challenger was found abandoned on Atmore Avenue in Carol Creek, not far from Creekside Park.

"Looks like he ditched the car in a hurry," Will commented through the speakerphone, "by the haphazard way it was parked. We have all available units in the area searching for him."

"Cardwell may try to access his grandmother's Ford Bronco," Hamilton said, assuming it hadn't already been seized as evidence in a homicide investigation. "Or he may be holed up at her place. Wouldn't even put it past Cardwell to hold her hostage, if it came down to using her as a bargaining chip to try to cut a deal to get himself out of this mess."

"I was thinking the same thing. Deputies have been dispatched to her house, even as we speak."

Hamilton wasn't satisfied that this would do the trick against an unpredictable and deadly foe. "I'm heading over there myself," he said. "At the very least, I'd like to talk to the grandmother, see what she knows, if anything. And when she knew it. As long as Cardwell remains on the lam, nothing's out of bounds as to what he might do next."

"That's true," Will said. "I'll contact Annette and let her know where things stand."

"Okay." Hamilton disconnected. He remembered that they had dinner plans at his house for this evening and more. He knew that Annette had also expected Cardwell to be picked up in short order, putting an end to his reign of Christmastime terror in the town. Maybe that would still be the case and they could continue their own agenda accordingly. But if Cardwell was able to somehow elude the dragnet they had out for him, then none of them would be able to rest easily. Much less enjoy the holiday season to the fullest.

I'll fill Annette in on any details I get as soon as I have them, Hamilton told himself. And if he found that Mack Anthony Cardwell was actually at the grandmother's house, Hamilton would make sure that, as the lead investigator on the case, Annette was in on any action that resulted in the murder suspect's apprehension or otherwise being neutralized as a threat.

When he arrived at the home of Vera Cardwell, Hamilton spotted two squad cars from the sheriff's department. He exited his own vehicle and walked up to Deputies Michael Jorgenson and Andy Stackhouse. "Trooper McCade," Hamilton identified himself, flashing his badge at the thirtysomething deputies, both around his own height. "What do we have here?"

"We went through the house and perimeter," Stackhouse informed him. "No sign of the suspect."

"What about the garage?" Hamilton asked keenly.

"Empty," Jorgenson replied. "According to the suspect's grandmother, Vera Cardwell, he took the Ford Bronco less than an hour ago."

Hamilton frowned. He had suspected this was

a possibility once Cardwell dumped his own car. They needed to double down on their efforts to locate the Bronco. "Is the grandmother inside?" he asked.

Stackhouse nodded. "Yeah. She's still trying to process what's going on."

"I need to have a word with her." Hamilton glanced at the deputies and down the street in both directions. "Keep an eye out for any possible sighting of Cardwell," he told them. "He might show up here again, if all else fails."

"We're not going anywhere," Jorgenson said, having already been given orders to stay put and safeguard the property that had now become part of a criminal investigation.

Hamilton rang the bell and the door opened. "Vera Cardwell?" he asked of the rather fragile-looking woman who appeared to be in her seventies and was holding a cane. She acknowledged this. "State Trooper McCade. May I come in?" She nodded silently and let him through. He took a glance around before homing in on a sofa. "Why don't we sit down?" he asked, wanting to make her comfortable. She followed his lead and sat beside him on the sofa, leaning the cane against it. Not wanting to beat around the bush, Hamilton said with an edge to his tone, as though she was clueless, "Your grandson, Mack, is in big trouble."

Vera's voice shook as she responded, "I'm not really sure what to say. Or even think, for that matter. This whole thing has been quite overwhelming."

"For everyone." Hamilton touched the brim of his campaign hat. "Do you have any idea why Mack would resort to murdering women?" He was aware that serial homicides were often rooted in something beyond the mere sport of killing. Or outright insanity, which he was pretty sure didn't apply here, given Cardwell's shrewdness and ability to perpetrate the murders successfully in a relatively short period of time by serial killer standards, while evading capture.

"Not at all." Vera frowned thoughtfully. "Truthfully, I'm having a hard time wrapping my mind around the things he's been accused of. This is so unlike Mack."

You clearly have no idea what he's like, Hamilton mused sadly. At least since he'd turned into a killing machine. "Was there anything in his background that might have led to this?"

She sat back, pondering. "Mack had a pretty normal childhood." Vera paused. "His parents divorced when he was still a preteen. That didn't go over very well with him, but he seemed to get over it. Same when his father, my son, Jeremy, died in a boating accident and his mother, Irene, remarried."

"What about relationships?" Hamilton pressed. "Has Mack had any recent breakups that left him bitter toward women, especially related to the Christmas season?" This seemed like something worth asking, as Hamilton understood that some serial killers targeting certain victims at a specific time were triggered by personal experiences that fueled their homicidal tendencies.

Vera wrung her hands. "Mack's girlfriend, Tricia Laborte, left him last Christmas for a man she met online. She moved to Australia and never really gave him an opportunity to win her back or adjust properly to the breakup." Vera's body quavered. "I thought he had overcome his disappointment. Now I wonder…"

I wonder, too, if this sent him over the edge once Christmas came around again and Tricia had moved on to greener pastures, Hamilton told himself. He peered at Vera. "We need to find your grandson before anyone else gets hurt. Including him."

"I know." She sucked in a deep breath. "I don't want anything bad to happen to Mack," she stressed. "I have no idea where he's gone."

Hamilton's mouth became a straight line.

"Did he mention anything at all to you that might be a clue?"

Vera's features strained. "He did say that a detective left her card at his apartment, wanting to speak with him."

"What detective?" Warning bells went off in Hamilton's head like sirens as he recalled Annette and Will paying her a visit.

"The one who dropped by earlier to look at my Ford Bronco's tires. Detective Lynley."

Hamilton's shoulders slumped. He sensed that a desperate and cunning Mack Cardwell might actually make a play for Annette. He got to his feet and told Vera sharply, "If Mack contacts you by any means, tell him he needs to turn himself in immediately!"

"I will," she promised him.

Outside, Hamilton updated the deputies and then got on his cell phone to call Annette and warn her about Cardwell. When she didn't pick up, he texted her. Then he called Will and was told that he, too, had been unable to reach Annette. Both agreed that she might be in danger and Hamilton arranged to meet Will at her house, while dispatching other law enforcement there as backup.

Inside his car, Hamilton contacted the Indiana State Police Special Operations Command and requested the use of its Emergency Response

Team and Patrol K-9s to assist in the search for Cardwell. Starting with the neighborhood where Annette lived, in case the suspect had yet to go after her by breaking into her house or in case they had a potential hostage situation on their hands. Or worse.

As he raced there himself, all Hamilton could think of was that he had fallen in love with Annette and she needed to know this. He would be damned if he allowed a serial killer to come between them and the bright future Hamilton hoped to build with the detective well beyond the holidays.

Chapter Seventeen

How did you get in here? Annette asked in her head. Had she forgotten to lock the door after all? She eyed her Glock 43 9mm pistol on the countertop. It was closer to him than her, but deciding that the element of surprise might give her the advantage in getting to it before him, she went for the weapon. But Mack Anthony Cardwell seemed to anticipate this and was lightning-quick in grabbing the firearm just before she could. He pointed it at her and said bellicosely, "Back up, Detective Lynley. Otherwise, I'll have to pull the trigger and forever mar that beautiful face of yours."

Realizing that he had her at a huge disadvantage, Annette complied and took a couple of anxious steps backward. Studying the man, she saw that he was taller than her and of slender build. His face was more triangular shaped than the digital sketch and his blue eyes a little wider-spaced and shifty. The black, short-sided hair was messy and the chinstrap beard not her cup of tea. He was dressed in all-dark clothing, from the pullover hoodie to the chino pants to the rugged cap-toe boots. She couldn't help but detect the noticeable scratch on his neck. *Bet I know where that came from*, she thought, recalling the DNA obtained from material Gemma Jeong had managed to gather beneath her fingernails after scratching her attacker.

Annette wondered if Hamilton, who was supposed to be picking her up later, had any idea that the wanted killer was standing in her house at that very moment. Or was this a fight she would be forced to engage in on her own?

"You know, you really should have invested in a good security system," Cardwell said with a sardonic chuckle.

Now you tell me, she mused humorlessly. When coming to Carol Creek, Annette had mistakenly thought she had left behind big-city crime. As such, she hadn't been in a hurry to have a security system installed. Her bad. Regarding her unwanted houseguest intently, Annette asked coolly, playing dumb, "Who are you and what are you doing in my house?"

Cardwell laughed. "I think you know exactly who I am, Detective, and probably have a pretty good idea why I'm here. After all, it's your sheriff's department that has a BOLO out on me and my face plastered everywhere for everyone to see. Thanks, undoubtedly, to that graphic artist bitch who got lucky and survived her date with death."

"All right, you've got me. I know who you are, Mack Anthony Cardwell," Annette came clean, seeing no reason for pretense at this point. "So, what are you doing in my house?" she demanded, as though it wasn't obvious that he intended to shoot her with her own gun. Or did he have something else in mind, considering his preferred method of murdering women was by ligature strangulation?

"I'm here by invitation, sort of." Cardwell grinned with amusement. "If I'm not mistaken, you left me your card, Detective Lynley, and asked me to get in touch. So, here I am, at your service. Don't blame me if I chose to meet on my terms and not yours." He laughed in an irritating way.

Biting her tongue, Annette forced herself to try and remain calm, so as to not provoke him just yet. "All right, you have my attention, Mack," she said, choosing to speak to him as though they were friendly acquaintances. "Are you here to give yourself up peacefully, so no harm comes to you? I can make sure that no one lays a finger on you and that you're given a fair shake while going through the system."

"Oh, really?" He kept the gun aimed squarely at her face. "And why would you do that?"

"Because everyone deserves to be treated fairly, no matter what he or she might have done," Annette replied unperturbedly. "It's no different with you, no matter what you've done." That hardly meant he should be treated with kid gloves. Like any other killer, he needed to spend the rest of his natural life behind bars and face all the discomfort that came with it. That was assuming he was able to avoid the death penalty in the state of Indiana for his capital offenses.

"Thanks, but no thanks." Cardwell snickered. "I didn't come here to turn myself in, Detective. Or maybe I should call you Annette." He laughed. "I'm afraid, it's too late for that." His eyes narrowed menacingly. "I came for you. In the living room," he demanded. "Now! Or I'll shoot you where you stand."

Unwilling to put that threat to the test, Annette had second thoughts about trying to grab the eight-inch chef's knife that she hadn't had time to wash and put away this morning and that now lay on the counter, near the sink. No, she had to be smart about this. As long as he was holding all the cards—or at least a lethal weapon, her own—she needed to play along for now. "Okay, okay, I'm going," she snorted. "Please don't shoot me."

"Good girl." Cardwell directed her toward the beige, round sofa chair. "Sit," he ordered.

Annette complied, as he kept some distance between them. "So, why the Christmas string lights to kill the women?" she asked, hoping to keep him talking. Like so many demented, overconfident killers, he probably liked to jabber on about himself. At this stage, buying time was her best weapon against the creep.

"Good question." He gave a short laugh. "To make a long story short, I'm taking out on other women the fact that my ex-girlfriend dumped me last December for someone from Australia who she met on a dating site. The Christmas string lights somehow seemed fitting, considering they reminded me of the note she left for me to find that was stuck to the string lights on our tree." He snickered. "Some Merry Christmas to me, huh?"

That explains why, warped as it sounds, he's strangling to death women this month, Annette thought. "Not to seem too analytical or heartless, but if you had such a problem with your ex, why not go after her instead of killing innocent women?"

"Well, truth be told, Tricia moved Down Under—too far away to go after," Cardwell responded tartly. "I couldn't leave my grandmother behind to fend for herself. Not the way my father did when he got drunk and stupidly killed himself in a boating accident, giving my mother a good excuse to jump ship, so to speak, in turning her back on me when she remarried. So, yeah, turns out my ex got lucky and others had to pay the price in her place. But don't worry, her day will come."

"Really?" Annette was weighing how to get him to put down the gun so his advantage would fall apart.

"Yeah. Once I'm done here, I think I'll head to Australia and take care of her."

"You really think that's possible?" she questioned. "You're wanted by every law enforcement officer in the state and beyond. There's no escaping to Australia or anywhere else. My advice to you, Mack, is to let me go, give yourself up, and this thing can end peacefully."

Cardwell gave a wicked laugh. "Afraid it's not going to end peacefully for you." He put the gun in one pocket of his hoodie and removed a string of Christmas lights from the other. "You're about to become my going-away present to Carol Creek. Once I claim you as the final and most prized victim of the Christmas Lights Killer, strangling you with the lights in my hand, I'll use your car to make my escape and work my way to Mexico and eventually

Sydney, Australia, where Tricia has set up shop and foolishly believes she is beyond my reach."

Annette watched as he approached her. Her brothers had always told her that the element of surprise was her best defense against an arrogant attacker. *Let's see if that's true*, she told herself, realizing it was either now or never.

While pretending she had surrendered to her fate, Annette waited till he was within feet of her, before she lunged at him, putting all her weight into it as she pressed hard against Cardwell. The momentum forced them both onto the floor, with her on top of him. She rammed her forehead against the bridge of his nose, drawing blood. He bellowed from the pain, releasing the Christmas string lights. He was distracted enough that she was able to grab her Glock pistol from his pocket and roll off him in one motion.

It wasn't until she'd gotten to her feet on wobbly legs, with every intention of shooting the serial killer, if necessary, that Annette grasped that he had managed to empty the six-round magazine and remove the round that had been in the chamber. Cardwell had shaken off the fall and nose butt and risen nearly as quickly, and was once again in possession of the string lights.

"Nice try, Detective," he said, wincing while his nose bled. "I anticipated you might try something stupid and planned for it. While you were upstairs, I took the liberty of emptying the gun of its bullets, in case it fell into your hands and left me in a world of trouble." He chuckled and stretched out the string lights, moved quickly toward her, and gloated, "Now it's time for you to die by strangulation, just like the others."

She found herself backed into a corner, quite literally. Her heart pounded rapidly as she contemplated her next move, short of being strangled to death.

IT WAS MINUTES earlier that Hamilton spotted the Ford Bronco Sport Big Bend that was registered to Vera Cardwell parked down the street from Annette's house. He tensed at the thought that what he'd feared had come true. Mack Anthony Cardwell had targeted Annette to kill. Hamilton tried texting her again and got no response. That told him she was in trouble and needed his help in a hurry.

He got on the phone with Will. "The Ford Bronco is on Annette's street. I think he may be at her house."

"Cardwell's inside," Will confirmed. "So is Annette. I just got here and can see them both in the living room window. The SWAT team will be on scene at any moment."

"So will I," Hamilton informed him and

pulled up behind the detective's blue Chrysler 300 sedan. He got out and rendezvoused with Will just outside the house. "What's happening in there?" Hamilton asked anxiously, his own view blocked.

"Cardwell's pointing a weapon at Annette, who's sitting down," Will told him. "They're talking. I'm sure Annette is playing for time while looking to get out of the dire situation."

Hamilton needed to see for himself. He peeked through the window and his heart skipped a beat as he watched his true love at the mercy of the lunatic serial killer. But judging by Cardwell's body language and loose handling of the weapon, which looked like Annette's Glock 43, Hamilton deduced that it wasn't his intent to shoot her to death. Instead, the gun was meant to keep her in fear till he killed her with his weapon of choice. Christmas string lights. *I can't let it get to that point*, he thought, pulse racing rapidly.

Working his way to the front of the house, Hamilton moved onto the porch quietly and tried to open the door. But it was locked. He guessed that Annette may have locked it after Cardwell had already entered the house. Trying to break the door open would only alert the killer, giving him every reason to finish what he'd started. *I have to be smart about his*, Hamilton told himself. Annette's life depended on it.

He rejoined Will and said, "Why don't you check around back and see if there's another entry point. I'll keep an eye on them and stop Cardwell any way I have to."

Will nodded. "Okay."

Hamilton found his way to the window again and peered through the glass. Annette appeared to be calm, in spite of Cardwell having her at a disadvantage. When the serial killer suddenly put away the firearm and took out what looked to be Christmas string lights, it was obvious to Hamilton that the perp was about to make his move. Pulling out his own SIG Sauer P227 pistol, Hamilton took aim squarely at Cardwell, when Annette suddenly charged at Cardwell like a battering ram. Or a woman hell-bent on going on the offensive against her determined assailant. She knocked them both to the floor, falling atop Cardwell, and then gave him a solid headbutt to the nose.

Just like that, Annette had gotten ahold of her Glock and was aiming it at Cardwell. Hamilton knew that she only wanted to hold him at bay till help arrived. Only, it quickly became apparent that the gun was empty. Cardwell had obviously and cleverly removed the bullets and was now back on his feet in a snap, with a bloody nose, the Christmas string lights in hand, and coming after Annette with a fury. *Damned if I let him hurt one pretty hair on her head*, Hamilton thought doggedly. He took steady aim at Cardwell and fired a single shot through the window. It shattered glass, and tore through the assailant's shoulder.

As Cardwell reacted, Will entered the picture, gun aimed at the killer, and demanded that he surrender. Instead, Cardwell removed from inside his hoodie what looked to be a Smith & Wesson .38 Special +P revolver and pointed it at Will, who took him out.

Hamilton raced around to the front door, which Will had opened, and went inside. Once the threat had been neutralized, he put away his weapon and ran into the arms of Annette, embracing her. "Did he hurt you?"

"No," she said, her voice shaking. "But not from lack of trying."

Hamilton eyed the fallen suspect, then Will. "Is he…?"

"Cardwell's dead," Will said. "He won't hurt anyone ever again."

Hamilton gazed at Annette, who was still in his arms. "I should have guessed sooner that Cardwell might make a play for you."

"There was no way any of us could have known that," she responded. "Cardwell was a loose cannon who had some crazy idea that he could strangle me and then fly off to Australia to kill his ex-girlfriend."

"That was certifiably crazy," Hamilton agreed. He remembered what he had been most afraid of: losing Annette before he told her how he truly felt. "I'm in love with you, Annette."

Will lifted a brow. "Say what?"

"We've been seeing each other," Hamilton confessed.

"Like you hadn't already figured that out," Annette quipped.

Will laughed. "Hard to keep many secrets in a small town. Especially when it's been as obvious as the nose on my face that you two had the hots for each other."

"Guilty as charged." Annette chuckled. "And, just to be clear, I've fallen in love with you, too, Hamilton."

He nearly melted, hearing those magical words. "Music to my ears."

"While you two sing sweet lullabies, I'll call this in," Will said.

Hamilton laughed. "You do that. And I'll do this…" He laid a kiss on Annette's lips, soaking in the moment where the future suddenly seemed a lot brighter, with a serial killer no longer able to come between them.

THE NEXT DAY, Annette still felt relief at having escaped from the clutches of Mack Anthony Cardwell with her life. Even better, she was in love with a handsome state trooper who'd finally professed to loving her in kind. It surely had provided them a gateway to the future that she couldn't wait to embark upon. Wherever this journey took them. But right now, she was on her way to Sheriff Teixeira's office, having been summoned for a final wrap-up of the Christmas Lights Killer case.

Will was already there when she walked in. Annette got a wink from him and wondered if he had spilled the beans to the sheriff about her new love interest.

"There you are," Teixeira said, smiling from his desk.

"Sheriff," she said evenly.

"Now that I have you both here, I just wanted to commend you for your work in bringing the Christmas Lights Killer investigation to a close. You two deserve a medal for ending this reign of terror on Carol Creek. And so does Trooper Hamilton McCade."

"Only doing our job, sir," Annette stressed politely.

"That's what I told him," Will said. "We do whatever's needed to accomplish the objectives of the sheriff's department. Stopping Mack Cardwell was just part of the process."

"Be that as it may," Teixeira told them, "we'll

all sleep a lot better now with the serial killer no longer a threat."

"Agreed," Annette had to say.

"Have a Merry Christmas and all that," the sheriff said, before dismissing them.

Outside Annette's office, Will commented, "So, you're off to Oklahoma for the holidays, huh?"

"Yes." She was excited to see everyone again.

"And are you bringing Hamilton along for the ride?"

She pondered the question. "We'll see how that goes. Hopefully well." She smiled. "Merry Christmas, Will."

"You, too." He grinned and headed to his office. Annette knew he had plans to spend the holidays with his latest girlfriend, a flight attendant.

She grabbed her handbag from her office and went home, remembering she had some packing to do.

"Juliet's killer is dead" Hamilton told Maureen in a cell phone video chat, while in his official vehicle.

Her face lit up. "Seriously?"

"Yep. We got him last night, after he tried to kill Annette."

"Wow." Maureen's brow creased. "Is she okay?"

"She is now." Hamilton grinned. "I told Annette I loved her. Turns out, she loves me, too."

"That's great." She beamed. "I'm so happy for you two."

"As you said, we both deserve to be happy. Maybe something good is coming out of Juliet's death for you and me."

"True." Maureen smiled thoughtfully. "She'll always be with us."

"I agree."

"Enjoy your holiday, Hamilton."

"You, too," he said sincerely.

After signing off, Hamilton reflected upon his good fortune in meeting Annette and what came next for them. He was giddy at the possibilities. When his cell phone rang, he put it on speakerphone. "McCade."

Lieutenant Tony Wilson, his district commander, said, "Hey, McCade. I wanted you to hear this from me first…"

"Uh-oh…" Hamilton was half kidding, but also concerned that his job aspirations had hit a roadblock.

"You got the promotion," Wilson said excitedly. "Just came in. You've been promoted to the Special Investigations Section's Organized

Crime and Corruption Unit, effective at the start of the new year."

"I don't know what to say," Hamilton said humbly, though he wanted to shout his enthusiasm from the rooftop.

"Your excellent work has spoken volumes for you, McCade. Believe me, I'm going to hate to lose you. But I know you'll thrive with your new assignment. You'll be reporting to Evelyn Guerrero. Good luck."

"Thank you, sir." Hamilton wished him a Merry Christmas and headed for Carol Creek, eager to share the news with Annette.

"That's wonderful!" Annette gave him a toothy grin as they sat in her living room. "Congratulations!" She knew how much Hamilton wanted the promotion.

He smiled generously. "It was a long time coming, but worth the wait."

"Some things are."

"True enough."

She gazed into his eyes, believing this was a good time to bring up the family reunion. "How do you feel about spending Christmas in Oklahoma City?"

Hamilton cocked a brow. "Is that an invitation to crash your party?"

Annette laughed. "I wouldn't call it crashing. But it is definitely an invitation. I'd love to have you there and show off my good-looking trooper to the family."

"As it is, I was going to ask if you wouldn't mind if I tagged along to Oklahoma for the holidays," he said. "Now that I know, the answer is yes, I'd be delighted to come and get to know your siblings, cousins and anyone else near and dear to your heart."

"No one is as near and dear to my heart as you," Annette had to put out there, knowing that he meant the world to her.

Hamilton blushed and put his arm around her shoulders. "I feel the same way. In fact, so much so that I hope to be able to accompany you to Oklahoma City as your fiancé."

"What are you saying?" she asked, holding his gaze.

"I'm saying that I'd like to take our love to the next level by getting married." His voice cracked. "Will you marry me, Annette Lynley, and make me the happiest man in the world? I realize we haven't known each other that long, but some things you just know feel right. So why wait, if you'll have me…"

Annette put her hands to her mouth, not having seen this coming. At least not before the year was through. "Yes, Hamilton McCade," she told him in the sincerest way possible. "No reason for delaying this moment in time. I would be elated to marry you and become your wife. And, whenever you're ready, the mother of your children."

"Then we're now officially engaged. With the ring coming just as soon as I can get it." His teeth shone brightly. "In the interim, this show of affection for my commitment to you will have to suffice."

With that, Hamilton laid a passionate kiss on her that left Annette seeing stars and counting the days till she was Mrs. Annette McCade.

Epilogue

With the infamous Christmas Lights Killer case put to bed and callous serial monster Mack Anthony Cardwell no longer able to target women, Hamilton welcomed the opportunity to spend time with Annette and her family in Oklahoma City for the holidays, prior to becoming an investigator with the Indiana State Police Special Investigations Section's Organized Crime and Corruption Unit. He'd gotten word that his duties would include, among other things, investigating organized crime with financial motives, political corruption and official misconduct by police officers. He would even be called upon to assist task forces in apprehending serial killers and other serial offenders around the state and elsewhere. He was more than ready to embark on this new direction in his ISP career, while leaving his days as a state trooper behind him.

But he was even more excited that Annette had let him into her life and given him the opportunity to find true, lasting love and build a relationship and family with. That included the extended family who came with the territory in linking with the Lynleys. Even if Juliet would never get to experience this kinship and loyalty, Hamilton was sure that her presence would always be felt in the building of bridges and the children he and Annette hoped to bring into this world.

"Go big or go home, right?" Hamilton joked after getting his first look at the massive two-story residence on Plum Hollow Drive that Annette and her siblings co-owned, courtesy of their late parents. Sitting on a couple of acres of prime real estate, it seemed to have all the bells and whistles, including a winding creek and a Roman-style swimming pool. The outside had all the traditional Christmas decorations and more. *They really went all out*, he thought, impressed. "Your family compound is a sight to behold!"

Annette laughed. "Mom and Dad worked hard and invested wisely along the way to be able to afford and spoil us with this house when I was growing up."

"I can see that." He could also see the value of keeping the property for the current and future generations of the family. Hamilton took in more of the place with its natural lighting through floor-to-ceiling windows, chef's kitchen, and a blend of antique and modern furnishings. A giant loblolly pine Christmas tree sat in the formal living room, fully decorated with lights, tinsel and ornaments. Loads of wrapped gifts sat beneath it in a scene that seemed to Hamilton to be straight out of a family holiday movie.

"Let me show you the rest of the place," Annette said eagerly.

Hamilton chuckled. "You mean there's more?" he asked, teasing her.

"We're just getting started," she replied with a cute grin.

"Oh, really?" He allowed her to take him by the hand and they headed across the hardwood flooring, went up the three-quarter-turn staircase, saw more neatly appointed rooms and went back down to the main floor, before Hamilton asked the obvious question, considering the various vehicles he'd seen parked in the circular driveway, "Where is everyone?"

"Good question. You'll see." Annette flashed her teeth mysteriously. "Come with me…"

Still holding hands, they made their way down a long hallway to closed double sliding doors. They opened the doors and stepped into an Edwardian drawing room with elegant antique furniture. Hamilton immediately broke into a grin as he saw a group of smiling people gathered around an enormous blue spruce tree, again completely decorated for Christmas. They had apparently planned to stay put and allow them this grand entrance as the newest couple and last of the family to arrive.

"Hey, everyone!" Annette uttered jubilantly. She was responded to in kind, before she continued, "I'd like to introduce you to my handsome fiancé, Indiana state trooper and very soon-to-be detective, Hamilton McCade."

"Merry Christmas, Hamilton," the group sang in unison as they gathered around the couple, first embracing Annette affectionately.

Hamilton grinned broadly. "Merry Christmas." He shook hands with the handsome and fit Lynley men and was hugged by the lovely, vivacious and equally fit Lynley women. It became abundantly clear to him that he was a welcome addition to the family. And for that, and being able to take the next big steps in his personal life as a devoted husband and father-to-be, Hamilton felt eternally grateful and ready as he'd ever been to fill those shoes.

AFTER THE WHIRLWIND family gathering, in which Annette couldn't have been more pleased at how well Hamilton was able to blend right in and was equally accepted as someone worthy of her love and commitment, they spent New Year's Eve at his cabin. He had thrown logs into the fireplace and built a fire. The blinds were open and they got to see the moon shining brilliantly on Lake Kankiki.

Annette was already thinking of ways to redecorate the cabin and make a retreat that was a reflection of both of their unique styles. *I have some great plans for this place*, she told herself. Hamilton was entirely receptive to the idea, wanting to make her happy. Which she wanted for him in return. They were even considering whether or not to make the wonderful lakefront property their full-time base of operations upon deciding where to live together. Especially once they brought into the picture children who could benefit from all the great water activities that would be available throughout the year. But that would be up for discussion later, once the demands of their respective careers were sorted out.

For now, Annette was more than happy to be engaged to the man beside her, who had his arm looped around her waist, holding her close lovingly. *If you never want to let me go, I'm good with that*, she told herself, feeling just as smitten with him. "I'm so glad we get to ring in the new year together," Annette cooed.

"Me, too," Hamilton told her. "Even better

will be ringing in the next year and the one after that and the one after that, and so on and so forth."

"You'll get no argument from me there." She imagined the day when their children would be gathered around them on such merry occasions. And maybe even their siblings and their children. And they could start the new year in different locations each year. How great would that be?

"Good. Because there's still one more thing left to do to make things between us official," Hamilton said, an intriguing catch to his voice.

"What might that be?" Annette looked up at him curiously.

"Oh, just a little something I picked up that I thought you might like to have." He removed his arm from around her and pulled a small box out of the pocket of his pants. He opened it to reveal a ring inside that he held up for her. "This is for you, my darling. I couldn't let the year pass us by without giving you the engagement ring you deserve as a prelude to the wedding ring, in making you my bride for a lifetime."

With hands to her mouth in shock, Annette took the ring from him. She would've been content to wait till he had more time. She gazed at the multi-diamond ring in 10 karat white gold. "This is gorgeous," she marveled.

"It'll look even more gorgeous on your finger, trust me," he told her. "Allow me…"

Hamilton took the ring and slid it on the fourth finger of her left hand. Annette lifted it up and watched as the diamonds sparkled. "You're right, it's beautiful," she gushed.

"So are you." Hamilton took her hand and kissed it sweetly in a continental manner. "I love you, Annette."

"I love you more, Hamilton," she said back to him, knowing that their love was equal in every way and promised a bright tomorrow.

"Shall we seal the deal properly?" he asked in a heartfelt tone.

"Absolutely." Her teeth shone. "Seal the deal as much as you like."

Hamilton angled his face and kissed her, this time solidly on the lips. Annette kissed him back just as passionately as the new year came in with a real bang and the rest of their lives began to take shape.

* * * * *

Look for more books in R. Barri Flowers's miniseries, The Lynleys of Law Enforcement, coming soon. And be sure to pick up the first title in the series, Special Agent Witness, *available now wherever Harlequin Intrigue books are sold!*

Get 3 FREE REWARDS!

We'll send you 2 FREE Books plus a FREE Mystery Gift.

FREE
Value Over
$20

Both the **Romance** and **Suspense** collections feature compelling novels written by many of today's bestselling authors.

THE NORA ROBERTS COLLECTION

40% OFF!

Get to the heart of happily-ever-after in these Nora Roberts classics! Immerse yourself in the beauty of love by picking up this incredible collection written by, legendary author, Nora Roberts!

YES! Please send me the **Nora Roberts Collection**. Each book in this collection is 40% off the retail price! There are a total of 4 shipments in this collection. The shipments are yours for the low, members-only discount price of $23.96 U.S./$31.16 CDN. each, plus $1.99 U.S./$4.99 CDN. for shipping and handling. If I do not cancel, I will continue to receive four books a month for three more months. I'll pay just $23.96 U.S./$31.16 CDN., plus $1.99 U.S./$4.99 CDN. for shipping and handling per shipment.* I can always return a shipment and cancel at any time.

☐ 274 2595   ☐ 474 2595

Name (please print)

Address   Apt. #

City   State/Province   Zip/Postal Code

Mail to the Harlequin Reader Service:
IN U.S.A.: P.O. Box 1341, Buffalo, NY 14240-8531
IN CANADA: P.O. Box 603, Fort Erie, Ontario L2A 5X3

NORA2022